Voices of Angels

Voices of Angels

A collection of fictional stories

Edited by Debz Hobbs-Wyatt
Foreword by Gloria Hunniford

Bridge House

British Library Cataloguing in Publication Data

A Record of this Publication is available from the British
Library

ISBN 978-1-907335-15-0

This edition published 2011 by Bridge House Publishing
Manchester, England

All Bridge House books are published on paper derived
from sustainable resources.

Dedication

This special book is dedicated to angels that touch the earth for but a fleeting moment. So softly their wings flutter before they are called back – but never forgotten. In particular to one special family who will never forget
ISABELLE MEGAN MARCHANT
Born sleeping on 9th January 2011

Registered Charity 1106160

The mission of the Caron Keating Foundation is to give a significant number of grants to small charities throughout Britain, as opposed to trying to raise money towards huge building projects or research which involves millions. They aim to make a difference by helping to fund pieces of machinery which detect faster, counselling services, many different types of hospice care – both at home and in the hospice itself – drivers to take cancer patients to and from treatment centres, complimentary therapies to help with pain control, and bereavement counselling.

www.caronkeating.org

Contents

Foreword

Voices of Angels is a collection of seventeen short stories by both new and established writers, all with one thing in common – they believe in angels – in one form or another. This is demonstrated by the range of stories you'll read here – from guardian angels to heavenly encounters, or even angels that are audited like any other worker! Some of the stories are sad, some are funny – all of them are thought-provoking. So whatever form the angel takes, the hope is that it will leave you to wonder.

After each of the stories is a special dedication by the author – to an angel in their life, living or passed. So this book helps us remember the people that touch our lives, even those no longer with us. Caron Keating, my daughter, being one such angel.

Caron was first diagnosed with Breast Cancer in 1997 when she was in her mid 30s. At that time, she was a much loved TV personality, having presented programmes such as *Blue Peter, This Morning, Top of the Pops* and *Entertainment Today.* She was happily married with two young sons, Charlie and Gabriel. After her diagnosis, she valiantly spent the next seven years fighting and managing the disease through a wide range of orthodox and complimentary cancer treatments. Tragically, Caron lost her tenacious battle with cancer in 2004 and subsequently my family set up **The Caron Keating Foundation** in her memory.

Caron always believed in angels – if she found an isolated white feather, she would always say, "That's an angel's calling card." Now when I find a white feather in an unusual place, I say to myself, "That's Caron's calling card."

She used to talk to the angels in her day-to-day life,

which I must admit, sometimes made me laugh. For example, a parking angel when we were desperate for a meter – and guess what? We always seemed to find one! I have to admit, I still use that parking angel!

It's lovely to think that angels touch our lives – even when we're unaware of them.

But sadly cancer also touches our lives – in one way or another. Through the experiences of family, friends and colleagues it has become a disease that no one can afford to ignore. Statistically, one in three of us will be diagnosed with cancer at some stage in our lives. However, survival is improving thanks to breakthroughs in breast awareness, screening and treatment, but there is clearly still much to be done.

The Caron Keating Foundation gives grants to all types of cancer charities, focussing on lots of smaller projects rather than trying to raise money towards huge building projects or research which involves millions. A donation from the sale of every copy of *Voices of Angels,* as well as a share of author royalties, will be donated to help us continue our valuable work. Like the foundation, Bridge House is a small publisher, a tiny team hoping to give voice to new writers with something important to say. They don't sell millions, even thousands of copies, but they do believe that like those white feathers that turn up in unusual places, it's the small things that make the biggest difference.

So we thank you for choosing to read this special collection and for lending your support.

Gloria Hunniford, October 2011

An Angel Named Dave

Shirley Golden

My best mate is an angel.

He appeared a month ago, just out of the blue. He wrapped me in his big old wings until I stopped shivering. I fought at first, battered against his vulnerable, fluffy bits, the bits that weren't fully formed feathers yet, the downy parts of angel which scattered into the air and caught under my nails: angel down. I'd imagine he'd create the softest, warmest pillows – heavenly. But I couldn't beat him off; he just held me harder. And I sagged into his embrace like a bedraggled stray.

After that it didn't matter where I went or what I did, his shadow, with its huge arcs sprouting from his shoulders, always followed me around, waiting for God only knows what.

"See. There." I point across the empty cans of Special Brew and glance to where Fiver is pegged out on the floor, his syringe emptied beside him.

He raises his head and wipes his nose with one hand, squinting into the corner of the room. "Hey, cool. That your man: Dave? He wanna shoot up too?" Fiver spends his life looking for converts. He doesn't like to be alone in his sin; plus it's an earner for him.

"I told you, he's an angel."

I named him Dave, seeing as he never spoke, advised, or told me anything.

"Yeah, right, an angel. Cool." His head drops, thudding against the threadbare carpet.

"He saved me," I say. And I take another gulp and let the can fall to the floor. I try a smile in Dave's direction,

11

but he's frowning and shaking his head. I blink away the double halo and pass out on Fiver's bed.

"Kirk, Kirk."

I can't work out if it's the door or my head pounding. I swivel my clock to an upright position: two-thirty in the morning. Jesus. "Who is it?"

"Who do you think? It's Ash. Come on, open the door. I've brought food and stuff. You OK?"

I push my legs to the edge of the bed and drop my feet onto the floor. What did she want at this time of the morning? I try to assemble my thoughts. Was at Fiver's. Left him unconscious and, when I woke, crawled across the hall. Sounds about right. Glow behind my head – must be Dave shimmering in the corner. What will Ash say? She's not as laid back as Fiver.

"My God." She drops the bag of groceries; apples and potatoes dribble out.

"Just an angel. Meet Dave," I say. I'm pleased I've evoked an angel, there's no other way to look at it.

"This place is gross, Kirk. Last time you said you would clean up, remember?"

She walks through Dave and pulls the curtain.

"Fuck." I slam my eyes shut against the onslaught of sun, bringing my hands to cover my eyes, and feeling like some monster Sookie Stackhouse's grandmother might be proud to know.

"It's one o'clock, Kirk, and you're still in bed. You're hung over again, aren't you?"

"It's too early…" I begin. But brain registers the significance of daylight: not two-thirty in the morning. Forgot: clock stopped three, no four days ago.

She pauses and surveys the room, one hand on low rise jeans where I can perceive a pinch of skin. "Last time,

Kirk," she sighs.

"Thanks, you're an angel," I say. Just like the time before.

"Who's Dave?"

I glance at the figure standing next to her, arms crossed, eyes sharpened like two blades pointing in my direction.

"Erm, was having a weird, God, just the strangest dream."

"Oh," she says. She turns away and begins to poke around in the cupboards for cleaning products.

She used to ask me about my dreams.

I retreat to the bathroom to douse my face, then I sling on combat trousers and a hoodie. Dave sits on the closed loo seat and watches.

"Why can't she see you?" I monitor his reaction in the mirror, but he just smiles; it's like having the Mona Lisa watching your arse. For the first time I don't find his presence cool or funny. "Can't I get some privacy around here?"

"Kirk? You OK? Who are you talking to? You want me to leave?"

He smirks, I mean actually curls those perfect lips like it's the best practical joke he's ever played, the big smug bastard.

"No." I unlock the door. "No, I didn't mean you. I'm fine, really."

Ash stands with dripping marigold hands and gives me a sidelong look. "Why don't you sit down for a bit? I'll fix us lunch."

"So, how's Chloe and Jess? Has Will asked you out yet?"

She flushes a little. "They're fine. They all said to say,

'hi'. Actually, Will and Jess have got it together, and Chloe is thinking about swapping to history."

"Wow, Will and Jess? I always thought... and Chloe, but she loved archaeology more than the rest of us put together." I was out the loop, more than ever.

"Well, since we've been in the field, she's not enjoyed it so much – you know her, doesn't like to break a nail. But you'll see for yourself soon. I know you'll be a year behind, but we could still meet up during free periods. You are coming back in September, aren't you?"

"Sure," I say and look away to where I catch Dave, eyebrows raised in disbelief.

And it's not just him.

"You've got to come back, Kirk. You can't just throw away your life. I know it's been tough..."

"I don't wanna talk about it, Ash, OK? You know I love that you come and see me. No one else does, but..."

Hammering on my door. "Sorry," I say. "I'll get it."

"Hey, is it good to hang?" Fiver pushes past me and stares at Ash. "You got visitors?"

"Ash meet Fiver," I say.

She nods in his direction and her eyes sweep across the month-worn, tea splattered t-shirt and stressed jeans, very stressed. They're marbled with a broken line of baked bean juice, or could it be dried flecks of blood?

"Hey, you haven't got a fiver, have you? I don't get my benefit until tomorrow and I'm desperately short." He wipes his nose with the back of his arm. For him there are two types of people: those you bring into the fold, and those to be used to fuel the demon. Clearly Ash isn't a potential for the fold.

Behind him I shake my head at her. He's not called "Fiver" for nothing.

14

"Sorry," she says. "Spent my last note on lunch for Kirk."

He shrugs and glances towards Dave. Please don't ask my angel for cash.

But he's off his high and doesn't notice the image glaring at him; in fact he walks straight through Dave, the oaf. He settles on the sofa and switches on the TV. He places a plastic bag on the floor where his hairy arm drops over it like a bolt. The bag bulges with cans. He doesn't notice how tidy everything is and how his feet soil the ends of the cushions. He looks like a bag of rubbish that's overdue for the bin men.

Dave and Ash look at me as if something should be done, but what?

"Well, I'll leave you two to it," Ash says, rising from her chair.

I want her to stay. I want her to say she can see my angel. I want to make her smile, like I used to. But the contents of the cans are brewing like an infection, pulling me into myself.

She says she'll come next month. She tells me to take care. She looks rather sad, and Dave fades a bit as she disappears through the front door.

I slump next to Fiver. "Don't shoot up yet," I say.

"What?" He's skittish, paranoid. "Why not? She the filth or something?"

"No, don't be a dick. Just look over there for me." I point at Dave, fainter, but visible. "Can you see him the, the person I told you about yesterday: Dave?"

Fiver's eyes skid about from me to the corner of the room. His knee spasms and his fingers tap imaginary keys. "Sure, Dave, the thingy, the angel. Right there in the corner." He smiles at me as you might a madman. Then he delves into his bag. "You sure you don't want another go?"

15

"Fuck," I say. "It's just me, isn't it?"

There's a glint in Dave's eyes that I don't like.

"Fiver, listen. Look again. Do you see someone? A person, a person with wings and a halo?"

"Far out," Fiver says and glances into the corner. "Perhaps I should change my drug of choice?" He plucks one of the cans from the carrier and holds it up to the light for a second as if he's discovered an artefact.

For once I don't pounce on it. I leave him to his latest enthralment and walk over to Dave. I prod him in the guts, but what a wanker I am; he's not corporeal and my hand slithers right on through. He doesn't even have the grace to shudder. "Get lost," I say.

The smirk is back, and I damn well know he isn't going any place soon.

I've never seen the inside of an intact church before – only the ruins of what once was. I mean on TV, sure, but not for real. It's like a creature you learn about but have never seen for yourself. Like the first time I saw a badger in the forest, and realised just how big they were.

Faith was for those frightened of death was how I'd always viewed it; for those who couldn't face the idea that they weren't too far removed from their ape ancestors, and random things happen no matter how hard you pray.

I'm struck by the coolness and stillness of the air. The light filters through the stained glass, creating an Other-worldly feel, which I guess is precisely what those medieval workmen were going for.

My footsteps create a tapping echo, accentuated by the emptiness of the building. Of course Dave's footsteps don't make a sound. But there's a rustle and a man in dark robes appears from the front aisle, like a bat rising from the rafters. He comes towards me in a flurry, never once glancing at the angel by my side.

"Can I help you?" He stops in front of me and uses the pew like a barricade.

How do I ask about visions without appearing like a mad junkie? Fiver's not got me hooked yet, but I know how I appear. "I have questions," I say.

The vicar runs a hand through greying hair and he glances at his watch as his arm sweeps back down.

"Is this a bad time?"

"Well, I have to... no, no of course not." He sits down, resting his forearms on the back of the pew and interlacing his fingers.

I glance at Dave; he's scratching his groin and chewing gum.

"Stop it!" It's a jerk reaction.

"I'm sorry?" the vicar says.

Dave shrugs and also sits down; he starts to blow, and a pink bubble protrudes from his lips like an empty speech orb in a cartoon.

I focus on the vicar. "Do you believe in angels?"

He smiles. "Why don't you take a seat?" He opens out one hand as an invitation.

I perch on the edge.

"Well," he says, "I believe in other dimensions and things beyond our understanding..."

"I mean, tall, golden-haired, haloed, big-wingy type things."

"I rather think that's man's generic interpretation of one," he says still smiling.

"Well, I've got one," I say.

"One what?"

"A generic interpretation – and he's sitting next to me, on your bench."

"There?" He jabs a finger to the side of me, spearing

Dave's bubble gum, which pops and leaves a sticky ring around Dave's lips. The vicar doesn't notice.

"Yeah," I say. "You really don't see him, do you?"

He looks a bit uncomfortable. "I'm afraid not." He pauses. "That doesn't mean to say you're not... not experiencing something."

"I can't get rid of it. Can it be exorcised or something?"

"Is it evil?"

"It's annoying," I say.

"Perhaps you need it. When did you first see it?"

"About a month ago." I don't tell him it happened when I was camped under the pier, high on Fiver's drug of choice. I've resisted the temptation of Fiver's produce ever since.

"Have you told anyone else about it? Has anyone else seen it?"

I hesitate. My junkie mate who lives across the hall just isn't convincing; besides he can't really see Dave, he's just trying to humour me while he keeps up the pressure. And Ash can't see him either. I'm not ready for the nut house yet.

He speaks more gently. "Do you have family you can confide in?"

Confide! He makes it sound like a dirty secret. Typical! Dave has cleared up the gum from around his mouth and is embarking on another bubble – a fuck off big one this time.

"I need to stretch my legs," I say.

We stand up and stroll to the back of the church while Dave remains seated, creating a record breaking bubble in the background.

The vicar is still waiting for my answer.

"My mum raised me alone. And she's, she's gone now."

"I'm sorry." He touches my shoulder. "She passed away? When?"

"No," I say tightly, my mouth working in defiance, in defence. "She disappeared about six months ago. I'd rather not discuss it."

He pauses and we turn at the doors and begin to head towards Dave and the bubble. "How about friends?" he says.

I suspect he's trying to palm me off, but the bubble has diverted my attention. Not due to the size, which is remarkable, but because there is writing scribbled within. Bold, gothic font: crash, it says. And then it bursts, big time, as if the world has exploded.

I'm falling as if through time. Sirens, blue flashes. Trapped. Legs numb. Cold, window open. Upside down. The world has imploded. Glass, scattered like jewels on the wet pavement. Voices. "Name?" "Kirk, Kirk, can you hear us, Kirk?" Blood. The taste of it, metallic smell. I can move my neck, but wish I hadn't. Mum, head twisted, impossible angle, resting against the safety bag, but not sleeping. Eyes fixed open. Whimper first, then scream. That sound, it's me, isn't it? Different voice: steady, calm, "It's all right, son, we're gonna get you out. Take it easy. It's all right..."

"All right. Are you all right?" The vicar peers at me. I pull back.

"I've got friends," I say. "People I can confide in." And I turn and run from him, and I don't look over my shoulder, not at the errant angel, not at the vicar, even though he's calling for me to stop.

Fiver asks me for the tenth time: "You can pay? This ain't stuff I can give away for nothin', man."

"I can pay," I tell him. I've the last of the cash Mum left me. I pull the box from under my bed. "This enough?"

His eyes light up like diamonds under spotlights. He sucks the fluid into the syringe.

"More," I say.

"You crazy. You're a newbie."

"You want this?" I wave the cash under his nose, as if he can catch its scent.

He draws in more and tells me to roll up my sleeve.

I lost Dave back in the church.

Since last month when he appeared and dragged me from the sea, he's been my constant amulet.

But now he's given up on me too. No more redemption. No coming back from this. Nothing to stop me this time. I hold out my arm, feel the pinch and sink into myself.

I never knew my dad; it was always just me and Mum, her fighting my corner, dragging me though the education system.

Faith, she'd always had faith in me – even when I flew off track. She juggled work and caring for me. She never once made me feel I was holding her back. Her parents were dead; she had no siblings. It was me and her, and she pulled me into adulthood kicking and screaming. And somehow, somewhere along the line I stopped fucking about, achieved good grades, applied for Uni. Just reached the stage when I realised how much she'd given – never got to tell her how much it meant.

I'm sinking, further and further, falling inwards, slipping. And the emptiness is good, like the painless moment before sleep engulfs you.

Bright lights and movement. Afterlife? No, don't believe in it, even if I did see an angel. Besides, it's too noisy. People shouting, metal clashing. And when I prize open my eyelids, lots of faces with masks and tubes. Hell, perhaps? No, don't believe in that either. Sinking and slipping again – bliss.

It's the voices that get to you first. And then something else, warmth around my palm, into my fingers. Dave is holding my hand. I try to speak, but something is lodged down my throat.

"It's all right. Everything's going to be fine now." The voice isn't convinced, even in my fog I sense it, and it sounds high and fretful, not at all as I'd imagine Dave's voice, more like Ash with a lungful of helium.

Now my throat's on fire, mouth dry. I blink but everything is hazed. My arm is an extension of tubes. There's a lump on the bed.

It's a head. It's Ash, her blonde hair dark against the sheets. Everything's illuminated because he's back: Dave, sitting on the end of the bed. We smile at each other and he winks.

Ash stirs, looks at me, wipes her mouth. "Kirk? How you feeling?" she says.

"Water," I croak.

She passes me a beaker and I sip.

"Why?" is all she says and she looks, not angry, but disappointed.

"It hurt too much," I say. "Where's Fiver?"

She scowls. "That waster. He left you, Kirk – panicked and left you for dead. He's no friend. Someone, I don't know who. Someone else in your block; I guess they must have seen the open door, and they phoned for an ambulance, and me."

I can't tell her just how unlikely that is. I can't tell Ash

21

I never wrote her number down, and I haven't had a working mobile in five months. So I reach for her hand and say, "Thank you."

"I didn't do anything," she says.

But she did: she's here, ever faithful – a friend I can confide in.

I indicate to the end of the bed. "I didn't think he could speak."

She turns towards the glow, but I keep looking at her. "It's my angel," I say. "You see him, don't you?"

She's staring off but her grip tightens around my fingers.

"Tell me you can see what I see," I say.

She turns back to me. The glow of the room darkens but she's close enough that I can see the tears caught in her eyes. "I always could," she says.

Dedication
For Roxanne, who's finding her wings

Shirley Golden is a novelist and short fiction writer, and her work has been accepted by magazines including Staple, Dream Catcher and Telling Tales. Several of her short stories have been placed in competitions including Earlyworks Press, Happen-Stance and Leaf. She is currently seeking an agent. For further information, please visit her website:
www.shirleygolden.net.

Blue Lipped Angel

A.J Spindle

Her lips are blue. I want to reach out and touch her, but I know if I do I won't like what I feel. Her body will be cold and lifeless. I sit back against the cave wall. There is nothing I can do for her now. It won't be long before I join her, wherever that may be. My breath comes out in puffs of white smoke and all I can hear is the harshness of the wind.

I wish I didn't have to die alone. I wish I didn't have to die at all, actually. Yet here I sit, wishing my last moments away. Willing the cold to take me under, to a place I can't be hurt anymore. It's gotten so cold, pain radiates in every nerve cell of my body.

I shouldn't have begged Morgan to come with us. Dad and the rest of the group are somewhere on the other side of the mountain by now. At least, I hope they are. I think about how we ended up here in the first place. How nobody knows we're in this ice cave on this side of the mountain. I shudder from the thought, or maybe it's just the cold. I don't know.

I look over at Morgan's body. Her black hair sticks out from under her purple toboggan. Her green eyes are open and unseeing. Morgan, just sixteen-years-old. My Morgan. I reach out with a gloved hand and close her eyes. Those beautiful, sparkling eyes. It takes all my strength not to try CPR again. She's too far gone. Her brain has been deprived of oxygen for too long.

"I shouldn't have invited you," I mutter to her. "I'm sorry."

I lay down on the ground and close my eyes, letting the tears escape me and turn to ice on my cheeks. I think back to how we got here. How it all started with skipping

23

school one day back in March.

"Hey, Gabe!" Morgan had said to me.

"Where'd you come from?"

"I took the bathroom pass." She held up the slip of paper and then stuffed it back into her pocket. "I needed a break."

"So you snuck out of Geometry just to see me?" I put my hand over my heart like I couldn't believe it. "I'm honoured." She flashed me a brilliant smile and tucked her hair behind her ear.

"I guess I like you or something."

"I like you too," I said. Her eyes lit up and her cheeks filled with colour. She looked embarrassed that she was blushing, but I thought it was cute. "You feel like skipping the rest of the day?" I asked.

"Maybe, if you can convince me. I *do* have a test to-day in fourth period." She pulled her lips together into a hard line, her eyes squinted. I laughed and so did she.

"How about you go back to class and ask to go to the nurse's office. Take the pass and meet me in the parking lot," I said. "Then I'll take you to Sonic to grab a burger and a milkshake. My treat, of course."

"Sounds like a plan."

"Then, if you're up to it, we can go rock climbing."

"Outdoor climbing?" Her face brightened and her smile made her eyes crinkle.

"Wouldn't have it any other way," I said. That's what attracted me to Morgan first, was her love of rock climbing. She wasn't afraid of a challenge.

I sit up quickly because the wind has stopped. Abruptly stopped. My head swims and takes a minute to adjust and then I just sit there. I look over at Morgan, still dead. I look away quickly and force myself to get to my feet. My body is stiff and moving is painful. I beg my muscles to

24

contract and release and they obey grudgingly. This may be my only chance to make it out alive. I don't want to leave Morgan, but I know she wouldn't want me to stay with her and share her grave.

I reach over and grab her pack from under her head. She won't be needing it anymore. She doesn't have many supplies left, but it would be foolish to leave it behind. Especially after I lost my pack in the avalanche that landed us here. "Anything can save your life up there, Gabe," Dad would say. "Even if it's just a candy bar. Hang on to what you've got." I'm not sure how a candy bar will get me out of this situation, but I'll listen to Dad. It might be my last chance to use his advice.

I push myself to the edge of the ice cave and look out. White. Walls and walls of white all around me. I stumble out into the storm and then realize I don't know where to go. Which way is east? I lift my boots above the fresh snow drifts and try to walk, but I'm too weak. I only get about fifteen feet away and then I collapse. The snow is in my mouth, up my nose, filling my lungs. I choke it down and roll over, exposing my face to the sky. This is a mistake. I should have stayed in the cave and died. It would be better than dying out here in the middle of a snow storm. Alone. At least I could pretend Morgan was there with me in the cave. Out here I feel exposed and utterly *alone*.

My head pounds. I'm nauseous and tired. I wipe my hand across my eyes and cheeks, like I can wake up from this bad dream, but when I pull my hand back I find blood on my glove. I wipe at my nose with my other hand and it's covered in red. Hypothermia causes weakness, confusion, drowsiness and slow breathing. Not nose-bleeds. What have I learned from Dad over the years? What else could it be? My thoughts turn slow, like a hamster in a wheel that realized he isn't really going anywhere. I do know one thing though. I have to get up, keep walking. I need to get out of the death zone.

I grit my teeth and force my body to stand. Morgan's pack is heavy, but I manage to throw it over my shoulders. I walk for a while and think of Morgan. The only girlfriend I've ever had. Maybe the only one I'll ever have. I think back to the day we skipped school to go rock climbing. How much fun we'd had. How I got my first kiss. How her lips were warm and soft against mine. I slip into the memory and I don't want to leave it.

"Be careful, Gabe! Watch your step!"

I didn't hear her in time and I slipped. Not far, but it sure did hurt. Then I said something intelligent like, "Ouch."

"Are you okay?" She climbed gracefully down to the ledge I'd landed on.

"Yeah," I said. "I'll live."

"You're bleeding." She pointed to my throbbing knee. "I'll clean it."

"Thanks." I've known Morgan long enough by now to know not to argue with her. She took out some gauze and white paste from her fanny pack and got to work. It didn't take long before I was all patched up.

"You have to be more careful."

"Yes, ma'am," I gave her a salute and we both laughed. Then it got quiet for a few heartbeats.

"Does it still hurt?" Her green eyes watched me carefully.

I shrugged my shoulders. "Not much."

She leaned down by my knee and kissed the top of the bandage. "Any better?"

"A little."

"Hmmm… what if I do this?"

She leaned in to my face and closed her eyes. Suddenly, I knew what she was going to do. I'd never kissed anyone before. How did this work? Was I supposed to

26

close my eyes? Pucker my lips? Tilt my head? They should teach Kissing 101 in school.

Her face drew closer and I leaned in. It was a quick kiss. Just a peck, but then we both sat back, shocked.

"How do you feel now?" She was trying to suppress a smile.

"Awesome," I said. Then I kissed her back.

I'm pulled from my memory when I hear my name.

"Gabriel!"

I turn my head and look all around but don't see anyone.

"Dad?" I call, but no one answers. Maybe I'm hearing things. I find a good spot to start descending. My gear was lost in the avalanche that separated Morgan and me from the group. I have to slide down on the snow to the narrow ledge below. I squat down and wrap my arms around a rock, jutting from the snow, and prepare myself for the drop.

"You can do this," I say to myself.

I move to the very edge and let go of the rock. I land with a thud on the ledge below.

And then I'm sliding.

I'm sliding fast. I reach out with my arms and try to grab something, anything to stop me from leaving the ledge. But my hands find no purchase and down I fall.

I don't even have enough time for my life to flash before my eyes, the way it does in the movies when the main character faces death. A large rock strikes me in the back and I cry out. I slide down and then come to a stop in a small packet of snow, my head hitting a block of ice.

My body is so tired and my back must be broken. It has to be.

"Gabe! Are you okay?"

I can't turn my head to look but I know that voice belongs

27

to Morgan. Which doesn't make any sense to me. Suddenly her face is hovering above mine. She's looking down at my broken body with her bright green eyes. Her cheeks are full of colour but her lips stay blue. If this is Heaven I want a refund. There should not be this much pain in Heaven.

"W-what are you doing here?" I ask through gritted teeth. I'm shivering so bad, my muscles seize and shudder without my consent.

"You fell again," she says. "I had to make sure you were okay."

"Are you an angel?" My vision is growing fuzzy. It could be a trick of the light reflecting off of the snow, but it looks like she has wings.

"Would it make you feel better if I said yes?"

"Maybe."

"Then, yes, I'm an angel," she said, her face grim.

"What's going to happen to me?"

"I don't know," she admits. "But I'll stay with you until the end. I promise."

"Am I dying?" I ask between gasps. I sound like a child. My voice soft and scared.

Morgan leans down and wipes a tear from my cheek with her warm hands. Oh her hands are so warm, I want to hold them, to rub her palm across my face and warm my nose and ears. I want her to hold me and keep me warm.

"It's okay," she says. "I'm here now."

We sit like this for a while and I can feel the cold creep under my skin and penetrate my bones. It's spreading through me, turning my blood to ice. Oxygen is scarce, so I save my breath. Morgan just sits next to me and holds my hand in silence.

"Morgan! Gabe!" A voice is carried in the wind.

"I have to go," Morgan says abruptly, looking over her shoulder.

"What? Why?" I ask. "Please don't leave me. I'm scared."

"I know, but I have to," she says. Her eyes run with tears. "They can't see me here with you."

"Please."

"I'm sorry. Tell them where to find my body. Tell my parents that I love them. Make sure my funeral isn't too sappy," she says with a slight smile. "I'll watch over you."

She spreads her wings, yes, those have to be wings, and takes off high into the air before I can tell her that I'll miss her.

"Morgan! Gabe! Where are you?" a voice shouts. It's getting closer. I still can't sit up, but I can yell.

"Over here! Help!" I cry with every ounce of energy I have left. I choke and sputter, and feel my nose bleeding again.

"They're over there! I see them!" someone shouts.

Within minutes, I'm surrounded by five people. Dad covers me with a blanket from his pack and asks me if I can move. I tell him I can't and he radios for help.

"We're on the East side. Be prepared with a stretcher and blankets," he says into the radio. "Looks like a few broken bones, a concussion, and altitude sickness."

That's what it was. Nosebleeds are a symptom of altitude sickness. Dad knows everything when it comes to mountain climbing. Dizziness pushes at me, making me more nauseous. I'm afraid if I close my eyes I won't open them again. But the pain is making my vision blurry. A blackness in the corner of my eye offers escape and I take it, leaving my body behind for the rescuers to care for.

When I wake up I'm in a helicopter. I can't hear anything but the whirring of the blades above us. There are people around me, but I don't recognize them. There's an oxygen mask tied around my face. I inhale slowly, taking deep breaths. I can't turn my head, it's been strapped down to a board, but I can see out of the window of the helicopter. The sky is bright and clear. I can see clouds in the distance. It's so beautiful. I blink and when I open my eyes again, I can see Morgan standing outside of the helicopter. Her face is smiling and she waves to me. I try to smile back, but I don't know if she saw. She blows me a kiss, backs away from the window and flies away, into the clouds.

I look around, but nobody seems to have noticed her. I wonder if it was all in my head. No, it couldn't have been. Morgan had come back to say goodbye. I wonder if I'll ever see her again. I wonder if they found her body in the ice cave. If they found her and saw her blue lips. Those same lips that used to kiss mine. I wonder if she's mad that I was saved and she wasn't.

My body is so tired. I close my eyes and picture Morgan as an angel. My blue lipped angel. I keep the picture in my mind until I'm too tired to fight off sleep a second longer. I surrender to my body's demand for rest. I take one last breath and use it to thank Morgan for staying with me until the end.

Just like she promised.

Dedication
In Memory of Sandy Kay Doud
An incredible wife, mother, aunt, nana, and friend who is loved and missed more than words could ever describe.
July 25, 1948 - April 2, 2011

A. J. Spindle writes middle grade and young adult fiction from her home in Texas. She is terrified of airplanes, loves pickle flavored sunflower seeds more than she should, and does not own a cowboy hat. Please visit www.ajspindle.com for more information.

And The Angel Wore Boots

Carol Croxton

Rosa was six when she first saw the angel.

It was the day after Christmas and she was walking in the hills behind their house with her father and her sometimes-best friend sometimes-best enemy from next door, Gabriel Roberts. Morning frost glittered and crunched underfoot and the sky was the blue of her favourite dress. A lemon sun sparkled on the sea and she was warm and snug in her new red Christmas coat, hat and gloves. One small hand was tucked safely into her father's big one, the other clutched Gabriel's and she felt for the first time a moment of perfect happiness that she wanted to keep tucked safely away forever.

Then she slipped on the icy ground, pulling Gabriel down on top of her and breaking her arm in two places.

That was how Rosa learnt to mistrust moments of perfect happiness. It was also when she first caught sight of the angel.

"He wore boots!" she said later, when trying to describe what she had seen to her mother. "He had blue smiley eyes and dark curly hair, with a gold cross in one ear, and a long white dress and big black boots."

"Did he dear, that's nice."

Her mother was more interested in trying to get Rosa's dress over her cast, something the doctor and nurses at the hospital didn't seem to have thought of when they put the cast on, so it's possible she wasn't paying much attention.

"And big gold wings folding out of his back. And he winked at me."

Rosa suddenly couldn't remember whether she'd really seen the wings, or if she'd added them later. She must have seen them, she thought, or how would she have known it was an angel?

So she looked for them particularly the next time she saw him. She was twelve and swimming in the bay with Gabriel Roberts. It was autumn, and the water was peppermint green and rough, so they weren't supposed to be swimming. But they were playing "hunt the dolphin" and you can't do that from the shore now can you? The sky was stormy, and shafts of sunlight lit up the sea like golden pathways to heaven. The hills surrounded them protectively, tinged with purple, and they splashed and swam until they were breathless and helpless with laughter. It was another of those perfect moments that she wanted to remember and treasure forever.

So when the wave smashed her against the rocks, breaking her ankle and slicing open her back, she wasn't really that surprised. Hurt, but not surprised.

It was the angel who led her back to shore. It certainly wasn't Gabriel Roberts, who'd run home shouting as soon as he'd got her out of the sea. Although in fairness that's why they got to her so quickly, and she supposed she didn't mind him being treated as a hero, since he brought her sour snakes instead of grapes while she was in the hospital. But it was definitely the angel who had led her to shore. He still had twinkly blue eyes, and dark curly hair and a small gold cross in one ear. He still wore a long white dress. He winked at her in quite a merry way, which she thought was a little insensitive given how much pain she was in. But perhaps angels see things differently.

"And he still wore boots, big black army ones. Why do angels wear boots do you think Mum?"

"I don't know, dear. Comfortable I suppose."

Her mother was more interested in trying to work out how to get the remnants of Rosa's shorts off without hurting her even further, so it's possible that once again she wasn't paying much attention.

"I suppose so. Although I can't imagine they have to do much walking, can you? Not with those big gold wings."

"No dear, probably not."

Although now she'd mentioned them out loud, Rosa once again couldn't remember whether she'd really seen the big gold wings, or if she'd added them later, lying in her hospital bed, waiting for the doctor and daydreaming about her angel. She must remember to have a proper look next time.

Next time she saw the angel, though, she almost forgot to look for his wings. She was 16 and it was the night of the big school dance. She'd almost fainted when Owen Davies, who was nearly 18 and played football and was going to be a mega-popstar, asked her to go with him. Of course she'd said yes. Gabriel hadn't actually asked her to go to the dance with him, had he? So she didn't feel too guilty. And anyway, it was worth it to see the looks on the faces of the sixth form girls when she came in on Owen's arm. And afterwards, after the slow dances held tight in his arms, when they parked his dad's car by the beach and he looked deep into her eyes and leaned over for that first proper kiss, Rosa knew that here was another perfect moment of happiness.

For a few brief seconds she really thought that perfect moments did exist after all. Until Owen's friend Bryn, slightly drunk on cheap cider, drove his dad's car into the back of theirs so that Owen, leaning in for a kiss, head-butted her instead, splitting her lip and making her nose bleed and cracking her head against the windscreen.

Rosa decided afterwards that the crack on the head was the reason she still couldn't remember whether the

33

angel had gold wings or not. But he definitely still had smiley blue eyes and dark curly hair. She'd seen that from the safety of Gabriel's arms as he held his shirt against her nose to stop the bleeding. The fist of jealousy that punched her in the stomach when she realised that Gabriel was at the beach with Nia Dawson probably distracted her from the angel's wings too. But he still wore a small gold cross in one ear. And he still wore a long white dress. And he definitely winked at her again. And – she'd looked twice to be sure – he was definitely wearing big black, very solid looking boots.

"Which for some reason seems stranger than all the rest," she told her mother later. But her mother was more concerned about whether Rosa had a concussion, something that had made Aunty Betty very poorly once, so it's possible she wasn't paying too much attention.

All of which has made Rosa very dubious about moments of perfect happiness. Which is why now, in her 24th year, as she walks down the aisle on her father's arm, she can't help looking round a little warily, wondering which gargoyle is about to fall off the wall, or which stained glass window is about to shatter.

She reaches the front of the church, and steps from her father's side to take her place beside her groom. Gabriel holds out his hand to her and smiles his special smile, the one that has danced in her heart since she was six years old. And when he winks at her, Rosa also realises that Gabriel has smiley blue eyes and dark curly hair and wears a small gold cross in one ear. Of course, it is she who wears the long white dress, and there isn't a pair of gold wings in sight. But when she looks down and sees the big black army boots sticking out from the ends of Gabriel's dress suit, Rosa begins to believe that perfect moments of happiness just might be possible after all.

Dedication

For my dad, Ron Mitchell (24 November 1932 to 20 March 2011) – the man who first showed me that angels do exist, even if they wear workboots.

After corporate careers spanning 20 years, Carol Croxton and her husband, Andrew, plunged into their mid-life crisis by moving to north Wales. Here Carol rediscovered a love of story-telling, stirred by the unique blend of myths, legends and landscapes of a place where the mountains stretch down to the sea and the sea stretches into forever. She has an MA in creative writing from Bangor University and writes short stories and novels with a touch of fantasy and magic inspired by her love of Wales.

Beyond The Secret Windings

David R Morgan

The story the wind told her
(For Jorge Luis Borges)

Beyond the secret windings she awoke from the deepest of sleeps, refreshed, to find herself naked in unfamiliar surroundings.

All around her seemed unreal, impossibly neat and contrived.

In front of her, a vast flatness, broken only by several paths leading away and out of sight, lost to distance. To one side, a sheer vertical stone wall, with perfect storybook cave entrances. On the other side, a pristine city of metals, plastics and brick.

She turned, and found behind her, a forest, thick with trees and plants, but with clearly defined trails. Finally, as she stood, she noticed beneath her bare feet that she was standing on a chalked circle, around these written words:

Beyond the secret windings, take the simple path.

She looked around again, considering all the paths available. Surely the simplest would be on the plains? With that in mind, she considered the three paths before her. One of clean-cut marble, perfectly smooth. One of flat stones, neatly sunken into the ground. One merely a trail of dirt, worn into the surrounding grass.

"The marble one," she considered, "is surely simple, for it is flat, no bumps, no roughness." With this in mind, she set off walking along that path.

She walked, and she walked. After a time she glanced back, and saw nothing but the path she was on. The forest,

36

the stone and the city were all far out of sight. And in front, the path continued, still, as far as the eye could see.

On she went, still, sure she must have chosen right. Eventually something came into sight ahead. As she approached, it became clearer: a stone wall. A city. A forest. And, in the end, a circle, with the words:

Beyond the secret windings, take the simple path.

Somehow unwearied, though she had been walking for what might have been days, she looked again at the flat paths. The worn path, she considered, is so primitive, so simple, it must be the right path.

So she walked, and she walked, not glancing back in case she somehow would be turned around, and eventually a speck appeared on the horizon. She approached, with trepidation, and again it grew: a stone wall. A city. A forest. And between the three, a chalked circle, and the words:

Beyond the secret windings, take the simple path.

"Well," she considered, "the stony path can't possibly be right, as it only shares qualities with the other two." She looked at the alternatives. The caves, simple, she supposed, in their lack of light and natural formations. The forest, considered simple by so many, yet boundless with complexity. And the city, simple enough to have been created by simpletons.

With no grounds to decide, this most logical reasoning having already proven false, she set off through the centre cave. She walked and walked, as the light drained into the distance behind her, until all was absorbed by blackness. She trailed her hand along the wall to her left, and walked, and walked, and eventually saw a speck of light in the distance. It grew as she approached, and eventually revealed, of course, the forest, the city, the plains, and the chalk circle. And the words:

Beyond the secret windings, take the simple path.

"How am I to choose the simple path?" she asked herself, "I have tried the easiest path, I have tried the least complex path, but still I am stuck here in this strange place."

Still untiring in body, though feeling emotionally aggrieved, she set off into the city, considering that the forest, like the stone path, shared simple qualities with the others, and added only its own complexity.

She walked through the gleaming streets, bright signs flashing at her, water dripping from rooftops, yet not a living thing in sight. Most of the signs merely advertised unpleasant food and drink, which, anyway, she felt no need for.

One sign caught her azure eye with its sheer plainness amongst the others, then held it with its words.

The way is simple. That does not mean it is easy.

She stared at the sign for a time, then walked on. She didn't go far before, on rounding a corner, she found herself back in sight of the stone wall, the forest, and the plains. A few more steps, and she was back in the chalk circle.

Beyond the secret windings, take the simple path.

She shrugged, and headed for the most overgrown of the forest paths. "Not easy," she said to herself, "but simple, in its way." And she walked, and she walked, pushing through branches, scratched and stung by sharp leaves, and still not a creature stirred, and not a breath of wind moved. Eventually, far from the chalk circle, the path grew easier, the branches thinned out, and she found the way much easier. She breathed a sigh of satisfaction, and started to walk faster. Some time later, she slammed to a stop, in horror. Ahead, through the branches, she saw the plains. Only a little further on, and the whole scene was again revealed, the city, the stone wall and the chalk circle. And the words:

Beyond the secret windings, take the simple path.

She walked to the circle, and cursed at the words, and screamed, "I have taken all the paths, and none have been simple, and none have led me anywhere, and all I have to show for it are these cuts and scrapes. Why? Why am I here? Should I return to the secret windings and search no more?"

And then she looked to the sky for the answer and then she smiled and she saw the simple path and she spread her milk white wings... and flew.

Dedication
Bex, Toby and Gemma – my angels who help me fly

David R Morgan teaches at Cardinal Newman School in Luton, and lives in Bedfordshire. He has been an arts worker and literature officer, organizer of book festivals and writer-in-residence for education authorities, Littlehay Prison and Fairfield Psychiatric Hospital (which was the subject of a Channel 4 film, Out of Our Minds). He has had two plays screened on ITV. His books for children include *The strange Case of William Whipper-Snapper*, three *Info Rider* books for Collins and *Blooming Cats* which won the Acorn Award and was recently animated for BBC2's Words and Pictures Plus as well as a Horrible Histories biography: *Spilling The Beans On Boudicca*. David has also written poetry books, including *The Broken Picture Book*, The *Windmill and the Grains* (Hawthorn Prize) and *Buzz Off*.

His poetry collection *Walrus On A Rocking Chair*, illustrated by John Welding, is published by *Claire Publications* and his adult poetry *Ticket For The Peepshow* is published by *art'icle*. David has two new books out in 2011: *Beneath The Dreaming Tree* (Poetry Space Ltd.) and *Lightbulbs In The Sea* (The Knives Forks and Spoons Press).

Afterglow

Maria Herring

Jesus had it right when he said, "They're buggers, the lot of them." Back then, I hadn't the faintest what he was going on about, but I've been around a bit since then. And as with all jobs, things start falling into place eventually.

I died when I was quite young. Actually, at the time I believed I was old – hurtling into my middle thirties like a steaming comet without any possibility of returning to the golden days of my youth. I had a job, a boyfriend, a house. Unfortunately I also had the belief that I wasn't happy because all those life-long dreams I should've achieved before middle-age hit (which was my thirtieth birthday) were still waiting to be done, and it was that which killed me.

Not literally however.

I was so busy in my head wondering where it had all gone wrong rather than, most importantly, where I was going, that I stepped out in front of the car and the rest of my life was truncated history.

Life after death had never occurred to me. But I'll freely admit that when I found it, I was relieved. There were no tunnels of light, or heavenly ringing of silver trumpets, or hordes of angels waiting to welcome me – that's just something the living like to tell themselves so the change-over isn't so scary. But the reality of it isn't scary either. In fact, it's somewhat anticlimactic.

Nothing happens. You stay where you are.

It's your perception that differs. Everything suddenly becomes clear and you can see for the first time. The living continue their unaware perambulation through life, but they're as insubstantial as, ironically, ghosts. But the dead see each other, those that choose to stay, that is. You can always choose to release your consciousness to the rest of the universe if you want to. That's another thing that becomes clear when you die – the enormity of existence and the power that permeates it. In general, most people who die after a decent life decide to release their consciousness and rejoin the power that started it all anyway, and there's no coming back from that. But from the rumours I've heard, you probably wouldn't want to anyway.

But those, like me, who died without warning have the option of staying on Earth. The official title is Big Guardian or Brother Angel (I confess, I wasn't really concentrating), but we refer to ourselves simply as guardians. It's very intriguing, after-living with people and watching what goes on, seeing what decisions they'll make. Because, of course, being dead has the advantage of being able to see all the various possible futures that result in a course of action all at once. Not the whole future, just the immediate. Contrary to popular belief, there's no such thing as destiny, only life. Yet there is such a thing as cause and effect, and any guardian worth her ectoplasm can deduce what will happen if one decision is taken over all the countless others.

Which was why the first words I heard when I stepped away from my body were, "I knew that was going to happen."

"Hello, Nana," I said.

"You never could pay attention, could you? Ah well, you're safe now. You're looking well."

"Thanks," I said, feeling a frown. "So do you."

She actually glowed. She also looked just like the young woman she was before marrying Granddad. I remembered the photos.

"I always knew there was a young woman inside me dying to get back out," she said, grinning. "And I was right." She gave me a big hug then, heedless of the ambulance she was leaning through. "It's good to see you again, sweetheart, but now I must be off."

"Where to?" Which was when she explained about releasing her consciousness into the universe.

"I'm hoping it'll be as good as that cruise I went on before I died. And I'm ever such in need of a holiday. You've worn me to nothing, my girl," she said with a twinkly smile.

"Sorry," I said, my mind all over the place. Unfortunately I chose that moment to look down at my old body only to realise how true that statement was.

"Don't be daft," said Nana, "I enjoyed spending the time with you. But I really must be off – one in, one out, you see."

I shook my head.

"We can't all hang around once our chosen one has died otherwise the planet would be teeming with dead folk. And that would just terrify the psychically inclined. But don't worry, love, Jesus'll be along any second and he'll see you right."

"Jesus?" I said.

Nana nodded, shone very brightly for several seconds, which would've hurt my eyes if I'd had any, then dispersed. I still sensed her somewhere, everywhere, and that comforted me. The paramedics who'd just finished scooping my remains into one of those thick rubber bags didn't notice a thing.

"Evening," said a voice.

I looked down.

"Down here."

I looked down further. Standing in front of me and grinning up like the cat of cliché was a little hairy man. If he had've stood on tiptoes and stretched his hands right up in the air his fingers may have tickled the underside of my chin. On his head was a mop of unruly black hair, and slinking above his eyes was its distant cousin, giving a new dimension of fear to facial hair. From his outlandish, outdated garb I could see bristling forearms that ended in fingers thick with spider-leg hair.

From my vantage point I noted an unsightly mound protruding from his back meaning he had to work even harder to look up.

I'd read enough fantasy to know that the creature standing before me was, in fact, a dwarf. Or perhaps an ogre.

"Hi," he said. "Name's Jesus."

The memory of my mouth dropped open. Then thirty-odd years of denying his existence came tumbling over me and set guilt gnawing at what would have been my bones. If I'd had any blood left, it would have rushed to my face and blushed it furiously.

"Don't worry," he said, waving a thick hand dismissively, "I get that reaction all the time. People expect me to look like this..." – his limbs and torso lengthened, becoming much paler and less hairy, his hair grew to flowing locks of soft brown-gold, his eyebrow became two, and his eyes turned blue – "...and as much as I like it, I wasn't born in Oxford." He shrivelled to his normal state.

He'd mistaken my shock however. "You're real?"

"Yep," he said, rocking forward onto his toes and then

44

back again. "But that's why I come to meet to everyone at this point in their death. I just want to apologise for the inconvenience."

"Of death?"

"No," he said, then chuckled. "You weren't a believer then?"

I hesitated, then shook my head.

"Well, that's all right then. People got the wrong idea, you see, and, um ... Well, it's all my fault."

He looked up from underneath his eyebrow and I gave him an expression of mild incoherence.

Jesus sighed. "I just wanted people to be a bit more groovy towards one another, and can you blame me, looking like this? But after those Romans did for me it all got a bit out of hand. I can honestly say, though, it wasn't me who started those rumours about being the Son of God."

"You're not?"

"Not even slightly! I was begot the same way as any other person on this planet." He waggled his eyebrow disturbingly. "But people don't take you seriously unless you make impossible claims like that, and I suppose I was a bit heat-mad – it's very hot in the Middle East every time of year, you know – so I let the rumour spread. And for a while it seemed as though people were being nicer." He smiled with one corner of his mouth. "Except the Romans, of course. And all that nasty business that came a few hundred years after. Christianity." He shuddered. "That's what I wanted to apologise for, but you never believed anyway, so it doesn't matter!"

"So you're not the Son of God?"

"No."

"Is there one?"

"What: son? Or God?"

"Yes to both."

Jesus grinned. "No to the first, and you'll find out everything in time, my dear, I promise you!" He turned and absent-mindedly waved at the departing ambulance that carried away my corpse. "So are you staying or going?"

"I think I might stay." I thought of my boyfriend, and really felt I ought to apologise for leaving so abruptly.

"Right you are. But just so's you know, you can leave any time you like once you've helped whoever you want to help. But you can't leave in the middle of a job. And there's no saying how long a job might take."

"How do I know who to choose?"

Jesus reached up and pulled my elbow so I was facing down the street away from where my accident happened, a tiny part of me marvelling how quickly my tragic end was cleared away. A cyclist rode through me and continued on without so much as a blink. There were people everywhere, all as solid as fog, getting on with their lives in the comfortable knowledge that they had all the time in the world to live it.

"Look at that couple," Jesus said pointing to a man and woman standing just outside a bar. "Really look at them."

I did. And saw that they were glowing. Her more than him, but they were both exuding a kind of light.

"The less they glow, the more help they need. Those two are pretty healthy. But then they're young and in love so they're bound to be." He cocked his head for a second. "But if they go into that bar they'll bump into his ex and she'll find out why she left him. But if they continue down this street they'll run into her soul-mate. Either outcome will leave him less than happy I suppose." Jesus shrugged and turned back to me. "That's all there is to it – pick someone and help. They'll not know you're there of course, but on some level they can pick up on your suggestions. Getting them when they're asleep is usually best for beginners. Any questions?"

I thought of my boyfriend. His kindness, his unfailing willingness to please. Then I remembered all those coupley things we did and never could again – no more late-night shopping, no dinner at his mum's, no walks in the park. All of those little things which, I suddenly realised, made me happy. Imagine my sense of surprise, then, when I realised I wanted to be sad but wasn't. My emotions had departed with my remains. Yet I knew I would be sad if I could, as well as I knew that my boyfriend was about to be. I needed to be with him. "Can't I just go home?"

"Ah." Jesus looked sheepish. "No. You can't move from where you were killed, unless you've found someone to help. That's the only way to get yourself mobile, I'm afraid."

"How do people get to be with their loved ones then?" I asked.

"Networking."

"That's how my Nana came to be my guardian?"

"Oh no," said Jesus. "You were with her when she died, weren't you?"

I thought back to that unhappy day in the hospital. I'm ashamed to say I'd all but forgotten about it. I nodded to Jesus.

"And very glad she was too. Anyway, I best be moving on. Best of luck with it all," Jesus said, offering a jaunty salute. Then he popped out of existence. Well, my sight, at least.

On closer inspection she was only a few years older than me, though she carried herself like scores of them weighed her down. I noticed her because she was hardly glowing at all. A burst of inspiration brighter than a solar flare told me she would be a good place to start.

I followed her. The movement gave me a funny tingling sensation.

She muttered under her breath, looked up to the heavens, and sped up.

Eventually we came to a block of flats that looked as uninspiring as their collective noun. Balding patches of grass plagued the front of it, a graveyard for broken toys, flat footballs and twisted shopping baskets. It wasn't a tall building, perhaps six or seven floors, but it spread out like a crouching spider.

She walked through the front door that was clinging to its hinges through sheer bloody-mindedness, and walked over to the lift. There was a hand-written note on it declaring it to be "Busted. Again." The woman thumped the lift doors and headed towards to the stairs.

"Stop following me, would you?" She snapped suddenly. "I don't want you in my home."

I stopped, looked behind me where no one was conspicuous, and then looked forward again. The woman was glaring at me, eyes narrowed and mouth an evolutionary step away from snarling.

"Yes, you," she said, even though I hadn't said anything. It certainly answered my question however.

"You can see me?" I said.

"Of course I can," she hissed. "You, and all your do-gooder friends. Which is why everyone thinks I'm mad."

"Oh."

"Now bugger off and leave me alone."

"But I want to help you." Even to my own cosmically-tuned ears, it was a lame thing to say.

"Then bugger off," she said, and stomped up the rest of the stairs.

Okay, I thought. I will. I'll just wait here for someone else to come along.

Except that wasn't going to happen. The further the woman moved away from me, the stronger the pull became, and despite my fighting against it as hard as I could, I was unable to resist being pulled along behind her. There and then I knew what it felt like to be a dog whose owner won't let them continue sniffing that irresistible lamp-post.

By the time she reached her apartment door, I'd stopped struggling. She, however, was oblivious to me, believing her order had been carried out. I think the fact I was still several paces behind her along the corridor, hidden from view, helped as well. Her door slammed.

That wasn't disturbing. But floating through it was.

The pulling stopped when I was in her flat. It wasn't very big, but the fact that the living room, kitchen and bedroom where all one area gave the place a feeling of space. It was clean and quite sparse – only absolutely necessary furniture lived here – but it was made untidy by piles of books, some open, some closed, lying everywhere.

She was standing in her kitchenette make a mug of tea, and I was standing in her sofa. I hastily stepped out. I felt I should say something to announce my presence but wasn't sure how that sentence should start.

"Um, excuse me," I said.

She paused, mid-bend to the shelf on the fridge that contained the milk. Very slowly, she straightened, then turned to look at me. "Why?" was what she said.

I looked around for inspiration but had to shrug the idea of my shoulders.

"I told you to go away!" she wailed. "I don't want you here. Your kind always talk to me at the most ridiculous times possible, and I answer because I'm polite, and now the rest of the population believes me bonkers! Why can't you just go away like the others!"

I shrugged again. "I can't. I tried, but you pulled me here." I thought quickly about what she'd said. "What others?"

"The others who came here to *help me.*" Her voiced dripped with so much sarcasm you could've bottled it and sold it to Americans so they would know it was a totally different substance to irony. "I suppose you *have* come here to help me?"

I nodded. "I wanted to apologise to my boyfriend for leaving without saying a word but it seems we can't go anywhere unless we have a chosen one to … pull us around."

A flash of possible sympathy swept through her eyes at the mention of my past love, but it was quickly replaced by annoyance. "Why me, though? Why do you always have to pick me!"

"I don't know … Because you look so sad?"

"Only because I'm hounded by dead do-gooders! Now go away, you can't help me."

A ghost of sigh escaped my lips. "I can't go *unless* I've helped you. That seems to be the deal."

"Well, the others all went when I told them to."

It's difficult to explain, but the moment she said that, the flat reeked of embarrassed silence. But it wasn't me and it wasn't her.

"Actually," said a voice, "we didn't."

"We couldn't," said another voice.

"Sorry," came a third.

I watched my chosen one's face slacken while her eyes widened. I turned and saw the living room was

50

almost full of guardians. Eight. That's a lot of goodwill, I thought.

My ward seemed not to think so. "You've been here the whole time?" she said.

"It's like she said," spake the guardian, whom I categorised as the leader, nodding his head in my direction. "We can't go anywhere until we've helped you."

"But ... I remember you from when I was a child!"

"You've no right to be mad at me, young lady," he said. "We could've helped an awful lot of people over the years, but oh no! Missy here decides to ignore all the sage advice we've offered her along the way because she's determined to ignore us! And the irony of it is," he said, in perfectly English tones, "is that we'd've buggered off and left you – much, much happier I might add – If you'd've just listened to us in the first place!"

In an instant I saw the tragedy of it all – how miserable she'd made herself, and how many people were still suffering because they'd been denied a guardian. "Sweet Jesus," I swore.

"Yes?"

The voice came from my knees, or thereabouts. The other guardians looked shocked; I looked down.

"Hello again," said Jesus. "Didn't think I'd be seeing you so soon, but no matter. What can I do for you?"

"Um," I said.

"Jesus?" said the leader. The man himself turned, then stepped back, startled.

"Good grief," he said, "what are *you* all doing here?"

"What are *you* doing here?" Everyone turned to look at the chosen one. Her face barely concealed her indignation and her body was actually shaking. I'd always thought people just wrote that in stories for literary effect, but this woman was actually doing it. I was impressed.

51

"Finding out why all these guardians are still here when there's plenty of work to be done," Jesus said, looking not the least bit perturbed at being seen by a live one. "And because I was summoned." He leered up at me. I shivered.

"So," he said, "tell me what's going on." His attention was back on the room at large, thank God. Possibly.

"She won't let us help her," said the leader. "And so we're stuck."

The not-Son of God turned his attention back on the chosen one, a look of annoyance furrowing his furry features together.

"But how did she not see you?" I asked, except everyone was busy telling Jesus why and how long they'd been stuck to the chosen one.

"It's not difficult, usually," said one of the other guardians. "Though we've had to work harder than normal to keep this one from seeing us. Most of the time we just hid behind furniture. Easier than concentrating on not being seen." I must have looked blank because he added, "You'll pick up eventually." Then he turned his attention back to the Jesus drama.

"So. What you're telling me," Jesus recapped, looking at the woman, "is that you didn't want ex-people helping you because you can, in fact, see them?" She nodded and he swung around to the guardians. "And you've all been stuck here because you've not fulfilled your duty?" They all nodded glumly. Jesus raised his eyebrow and folded his arms across his chest. "Quite a situation we've got here."

"What do we do?" I asked.

Jesus shrugged.

"Don't I get the choice?" the woman asked. "I was happy enough before all this lot came along." She indicated the shuffling group of ghosts in her living room.

"Obviously not," said Jesus, "or they wouldn't have picked you."

She huffed. "Well, you're Jesus! Can't you do something about it?"

He looked sheepish. "Doesn't quite work like that ... You'll understand once you're dead."

Her eyes widened and a small, strangled noise escaped from her throat.

"Which isn't yet, don't worry," he said, in tones which conveyed he wasn't. He looked around for a bit, tapped his foot soundlessly, and muttered under his breath. "The only way out of this," he said eventually, "is to let them do their job. You're going to have to let them" – he jerked his thumb towards us – "advise you. They'll go then. And once they've all gone, you're going to have to make an effort to be happy otherwise you'll be followed for the rest of your life."

"But how are we supposed to do that?" We all said at once.

Jesus opened his mouth, then shut it again. Finally he said, "Not my problem. You try and help the living as much as you can, but do they ever think to thank you? Always finding the worst in a situation... or taking a perfectly good idea and ruining it. They're buggers, the lot of them."

And with that, he vanished.

"I wouldn't eat that apple if I were you," said another guardian. "It's rotten. It'll make you sick."

The chosen one looked at the apple, then the guardian. Without taking her eyes off him, she threw it in the bin. It missed and splashed across the floor but she ignored it.

The guardian disappeared in a haze of white light.

"Five down, four to go," she said.

It wasn't the best way to use the wisdom of angels, I thought, but none of us wanted to argue with her any more. The first had gone by suggesting she walk to work instead of catching the bus. That had turned out to be fortuitous because there was a strike on, and she was the only one who'd arrived at work on time. Her boss was happy about that, and remembered her dedication.

The second simply told her to take a bath instead of a shower.

The third told her to say "Hello" to the old woman who lived below her.

The fourth suggested she call her mum for a chat.

When you're dead, time doesn't mean anything any more, it's just an arbitrary word defining a human perception; but a week had gone by and I still didn't know how to advise this woman in order to help her. I wanted to really help her, not just escape as quickly as possible. But there was still a large part of me that was desperate to get to my boyfriend and apologise for never coming home.

I had to stop being selfish though. I'd never come up with anything if I didn't focus my ghostly mind.

For another two weeks the rest of us were pulled along like errant children reluctant to go to school as she went to work, or perhaps shopping, and then back home again. I kept my mind open, but could see nothing that might cause her any real benefit. She was satisfied in her job; she simply wanted something that allowed her to pay the bills. She had no ambition, and that was something I couldn't change.

The others were getting restless, saying things like, "I wouldn't make that cup of tea if I were you" but to no avail.

The sixth guardian was just pure lucky. The chosen one was lost in thought on her way home from work, and went to cross the road – into the path of cyclist. He would've had to swerve in order to avoid her, throwing himself in the path of an oncoming car. But the guardian shouted "Stop!" in time, and when she did, he vanished. Looking surprised and pleased with himself at the same time.

"Why don't you ever go out?" whined the seventh guardian one evening. "It'd make the process a lot quicker if you were interacting with other people, you know."

"I don't want to go out," she said. "I've got too many books to read. Now shush."

Eventually the seventh departed by advising she make a suggestion at work about the filing system. She did, and he left, but not without knowing that it'd get her irrefutably noticed by the boss (who still remembered her turning up early on the day of the strike). This resulted in a promotion and pay-rise. She grumbled to me and number eight about it, but we clearly saw she was secretly happy.

The eighth guardian took his cue from that and advised another career-stimulating suggestion.

"She'll be team leader before you know it," he said to me before vanishing.

"Just you and me now," the chosen one said on a sunny Sunday afternoon.

I nodded. And my mind blossomed with an idea. "I think you should go for a walk in the park."

"Now?"

"Why not? It's a beautiful day."

"You're right. Let's go."

Over the weeks she'd changed considerably. She stood up straighter when she walked, she thought longer about what to wear after having shopped for new clothes with her higher salary. She was even meeting the girls from the office for drinks once or twice a week. When we stepped out into the glorious summer day, her aura shone brighter than the sun. I was pleased for her.

"I haven't been to the park for an age," she whispered as we walked along the street.

"It's a beautiful place to spend a sunny afternoon," I said.

She nodded, looked at me and smiled. She was actually a very pretty woman now that her perceptions about life and after-death had changed.

"I used to come here all the time," I said. "It's one of my favourite places. Especially the lake."

"Well that's where we should go now, then."

I nodded again and smiled. She didn't even notice that the other park pedestrians looked at her strangely for talking to no one. Or if she did, she didn't care any more.

The lake came into view, as bright and blue as ornamental glass. Swans swept majestically across it, not deigning to look at the common folk clustered around the banks. Some were sitting in groups, chatting; others were throwing scraps of food out to the ducks. All of them had the bright glow of people enjoying the very moment.

Except for one. One man. He stood out like a snuffed-out candle in a hall full of lit ones. And if my heart had've still been in my chest it would've lurched up into my non-existent mouth.

It was him. The man I'd left for no reason other than a wandering mind; the man I hadn't said sorry to yet; the man I used to love. There he was, sitting in our old spot where the grass bank dipped down and the lake lapped up against the sliver of sand.

And he was so sad.

Being dead, I was completely unable to feel emotions

56

any longer, but I hadn't been dead for that long and I could remember pity and regret. I remembered them now, stronger than the sun and deeper than the lake.

I heard my chosen one gasp; she'd just noticed him. "The poor man," she whispered. "He looks so distraught."

There were many things I wanted to say to him, but I knew he wouldn't hear them. I wanted to hold him one last time, but I knew he wouldn't feel me. Life, after all, is solely for the living.

Yet I saw a future for him... One where his aura glowed more brilliantly than all others, and I wanted him to have it.

I looked at my chosen one, sympathy etched across her face. "I think you should go and talk to him," I said.

Then I vanished.

Dedication
To the angel in my life- my Nana, Audrey Herring. She's always there to support and encourage me, and her strength and constant optimism will inspire me forever. Plus, she makes the best cakes!

Maria Herring is a travelling English teacher, currently living in Lyon, but she has decided to swap the whiteboard for a laptop. Because, as it turns out, writers can work anywhere in the world as well. She's older than she ever intended to be but can't deny she's had a lot of fun along the way.

The Watcher

Sarah Evans

Mychal has been following them now for several days, sometimes shadowing her, stepping into the spaces her feet leave behind, sometimes trailing her companion. Tonight it is the two of them.

They walk together separately, an open space between their shoulders. Mychal senses how each of them is unhappy, the emotions spreading softly out, blurring the boundaries set by bodies and clothes.

The woman is fuelled by spurts of hugged-in anger, her arms fixing across her chest before they loosen to a dangling despair. The man's unhappiness is threaded through with longing, and his arm arcs towards the woman at his side, as if he might catch her hand, then slumps back against his thigh. They walk into the yellow light pooling beneath a streetlamp, and Mychal watches as the man's face turns to look at her, while her face remains resolutely forward.

It is their sadness which draws Mychal in.

The street teems with bodies, which flow around the couple, like water coursing past an island in a stream. Mychal follows closely in the couple's wake, maintaining his focus, not allowing the distraction into other people, other stories. He'd like to see this one through.

Their footsteps slow outside a brightly blue-lit facade. The man speaks: "How about here?" And she says, "yes."

The man pulls open the heavy glass door then lets the woman walk before him, her shoulder brushing his. His arm drops the door, then curves behind – close to, but not touching – her narrow back, in a gesture of protection which she doesn't see. Inside is crowded, the space dense with the ricochet of choppy feelings. Generally Mychal avoids bars with their volatile moods, the alcohol agitating and intensifying things. He wishes the couple had not come here, wishes that the woman had agreed to the man's earlier suggestion that they go somewhere quiet. But the woman brushed this off. She needed cheering up, she said, somewhere lively. Except now as her eyes cast round the liveliness of groups and couples, her unhappiness swells, billowing gently outwards from the contours of her body.

They sit tightly in a corner, and Mychal edges in beside them, close enough that he could touch, except they would not feel him.

The man heads briskly for the bar, and Mychal catches the flash of relief, as if being so close to her is too much strain. The woman keeps her eyes down, while her fingers pick at broken nails and she settles into despondency. The man returns, carrying two glasses. His eyes are trained on her, while she continues staring down at the smeared table, and her fingers fray the beer mat. She looks up only as the man's shadow casts over her, her melancholy in no way eased by his approach. The man's emotions are more complex, lifting at the sight of her pale beauty, collapsing down in uncertainty. The rise and fall of his sadness is like waves breaking on a beach, constantly it ebbs and flows.

"Thanks," she says, as her smile mimics levity.

"Cheers." The man lifts his glass on an uplift to his up/down mood.

The evening pauses.

"So," the man says. "D'you want to talk?"

"I don't know."

Mychal knows how it will go. People rarely say the things they want to, or that they mean. He learns by watching and by his ability to sense the emotions which seep beyond the boundaries of skin, shifting the texture of the surrounding air.

59

"Talking about it might help," the man persists.

"It won't change anything though, will it?"

Her words are face-slap sharp and the man shrinks back from her. Mychal feels his own slight recoil. It is hard observing unhappiness like this. He leans in towards the woman, his form passing over her, wishing he might reach across the veil which separates his world from theirs and offer his own understanding. But it is difficult.

"I'm sorry." The woman's voice softens and the man reaches across the table and his fingers caress the back of her hand. He beats with joy when she doesn't move her hand away.

"What is there to say?" she asks. "Stuart's shagging someone else."

The man flinches back again, seeking distance from her bitterness. His mouth opens, but then he remains silent and apprehension shimmers.

"Which I suppose makes me an idiot," she carries on, and the anger which has been radiating outwards in needle tendrils, now turns round and redirects inwards. The man moves his hand to touch her shoulder and gazes at her closed face. She does not look back at him, and his unspoken pleading remains as invisible to her as Mychal does.

"Don't," the man says, and his feelings are all tangled up: the pulsing joy of being with her, of touching her, the spikes of pain at seeing her unhappy and his own unspoken torment, his anger towards this other man and the fact he is furtively pleased. "He isn't worth it."

Her fury spurts in shards in all directions. "I know. I'm stupid. But that doesn't stop..." And then the shards shatter and her voice deserts her. "It just hurts," she says quietly. "It hurts."

Her eyes flood, and she blinks them vigorously and the

man edges in closer. He spreads his arm across and down her back, his hand curving over her ribs to alight on her waist. He draws her in towards him. Her head drops onto his shoulder and her body slumps into the small comfort that he offers, while optimism is bubbling out and around him and mingling with the flaring of desire.

"I'm sorry," she says, as she sniffles loudly.

"It's OK." His fingers stroke her hip, and while his voice is soothing and subdued, happiness froths.

She pulls back, wipes her tears brusquely away with the back of her hand and then delves into her bag to find a tissue. She's hot and sharp-edged with embarrassment. "Sorry!" she insists again, not seeing how the man's hope is dropping back now into gloom as he loosens his hold.

It is wearing, Mychal thinks, the constant shifting of moods, and his own careful observance of them.

"He says he's sorry," the woman says, her voice more controlled now.

"I'm sure he does." The man's voice is harder, as his arm retreats completely.

"Says it was a mistake. It won't happen again."

"No." The man pauses, tense with fighting back against his impulse, then giving in. "He would say that wouldn't he?"

Her lips press together. Her anger spears towards her companion now. "You don't know him."

It's the man's turn to switch into fury now. "I know enough. I know he doesn't make you happy."

"You don't know that."

"Time and again, you tell me this stuff. He's always letting you down. Never there when you need him. He doesn't deserve you. And now this."

"It was only the once. It won't happen again."

"So he says."

Her fingers clench round the glass and her whole body is rigid. The man beside her is unyielding too, tensing like a sprinter on the starting block.

Mychal sees how it could go. Those serpent tight fingers might raise the glass and throw the contents over the man who sits beside her, substituting her anger, and he, furious with misery, would jerk away and leave.

Mychal would like to intervene. It's not impossible. He tries to send his consciousness out, to let it wrap around them, to make his presence felt.

The man slackens to weariness. "I'm sorry," he says. "You're right. I don't know him. I shouldn't have said that. I just don't like to see you unhappy."

It's her turn to unfurl now, and she drinks deeply. "No, I'm sorry. I'm not much company. Don't know how you put up with me."

The man withdraws into a haze of misery. He replays, but briefly, his gesture of earlier, extending his arm across her shoulder, hugging her, then letting go. "Another drink?" he asks.

She tosses back the remains of her glass and a foamy giddiness emanates from her. "It's my turn. Let me get them."

"No," he insists. "I invited you. Let me." And walking to the bar his step springs, as if pleased by this small act of persuasion.

The evening swings into a rhythm. They drink. They banter back and forth: gossip about mutual acquaintances at work, the film they saw separately, programmes on TV. Mychal's attention drifts and he skims the surfaces of those around him.

Unhappiness is not unusual.

The couple lapse again to silence and Mychal focuses back.

"Perhaps it isn't such a big deal," she says eventually,

talking flatly now, the heat of emotion dulled by the cold wine.

The man's throat tightens as he swallows back. Mychal watches the man watching her; he can see the mist of tenderness mingling with the sparks of desire and pins of rawness. The man's eyes track hers, asking, pleading that she look properly at him. But for all her eyes move and flicker across the man's face, then out across the dim-lit crowded space and down to her fingernails clutching at the table edge, she remains unseeing. Mychal would like to cross the screen between their spheres, and to lift for her the gauze through which she sees only the superficial features of the man beside her.

"It's only sex." She laughs, and the sound emerges harsh and grating.

The man's lips are taut with holding in all he'd like to say.

"It was only once." Her fingers flick at the air, trying to flick away the dense fog of misery.

The man remains still and quiet, refusing to acquiesce, fearful at disagreeing.

"Maybe I should find a pick-up for the night, get my own back and then we can move on," she muses, her fingers tapping the table, and just for a moment her mood lightens, mellowing with the wine, as if she really has alighted on a solution.

"One way of looking at it." The man finally speaks, his words accompanied by a fierce pulse of lust, which is mingled with anger and devoid of any of his earlier tenderness. Then he scrapes his stool back and his voice reverts to neutral as his legs uncoil to standing and he offers to buy her another drink.

Some time later, they leave the bar. Mychal feels the relief of the broad expanse of sky.

63

"Look," the man says and he touches the woman's arm, while his other hand gestures upwards. The heavens are scattered with stars and though they must have seen this many times, both share a moment's awe. "The North Star," the man says, his finger pointing to the brightest, and she laughs and says she's never understood the constellations so he traces out the obvious ones, giving her their names. "Doesn't look much like a lion," she says, and both relax a little.

"Where next?" he asks, and he glows with the fleeting happiness of her arm linked to his and both of them gazing at the stars.

"It's late," she says. "I should get back..." Her voice trails.

"Not that late." He speaks quickly then hesitates.

"It's just..." The woman's voice crumples. "It's stupid. I don't want to go back to mine. His stuff is all over the place. Reminders everywhere. It's even possible he'll be there; he still has keys." Her emotions are confused, wanting/not wanting the possibility she's just considered. "And I know I have to face it, except I can't. Not just now."

"We could stroll," the man says, though both of them are shivering. "Find a night club. An all night café." But he fails to inject enthusiasm for these things. "Or..." and the pause lingers, as he's caught between hope and despair. "You could come back to mine." He says it lightly, a teasing suggestion, but fails to expel the note of longing. "I mean..." he falters. "I don't mean..."

Except it's clear, of course, he does.

They are back now, at the man's flat. The woman follows him into the beige/brown space and Mychal follows close behind.

The woman treads slowly, hunched down by her misery. Her eyes click round and take in the grubby magnolia walls, the MDF shelves, the sagging sofa.

"This is nice," she says too brightly and so conveying just the opposite.

Mychal catches the spreading dismay in the man, as his eyes scan, seeing the dreary décor through her eyes. "Could do with updating." He takes the woman's coat and as he goes to hang it up, he buries, for a moment, his face in its lining.

"Coffee?" the man offers, but the woman just smiles back, sharp and brittle, and she repeats the word – "coffee?" – as a mocking question.

Desire lurches hard and fast in the man's body.

He looks at her, unsmiling, uncertain. He steps closer, anxiety keening with the narrowing of the gap, mingling with the force of wanting.

The woman is uncertain too.

The space between them closes and the man is leaning out towards her, wanting to pitch forward and trust that she will catch him.

Mychal watches, his own yearning mingling with that of these strange beings whom he shadows.

The man's mouth closes against the woman's, his primary response that of relief that she does not immediately deflect him. In the woman, Mychal senses a different form of relief, a letting go, an abandonment into the moment.

Mouths bruise together. Teeth clatter against teeth. Bodies squeeze tight. Hands start slow, then are suddenly busy, moving over, then seeking ways to burrow under clothes.

Amidst the heat, Mychal catches the man's wingbeat of confusion followed by him abruptly pulling back.

65

Everything is mixed up. Hunger. Happiness. Doubt.

The man presses his forehead against hers, his breath hard and fast.

"You're sure?" he says.

It's her turn now to waver, and the man's emotions shift to apprehension, while desire presses harder.

Then she reaches up, and this time her kiss is slower, gentler, drawing both of them more fully into this, into the awareness of nothing but themselves and of each other.

The man manoeuvres the two of them, awkwardly, to the bedroom. Mychal is indifferent to the struggling out of clothes and to the ways the two of them cast about with fingers, lips and tongues, and limbs. Indifferent to the groans and the sound of flesh suckering against flesh. He seeks through the blaze of passion, alert to other feelings which surface and submerge. Flashes of tenderness. Needles of discomfort. Bubbles of amusement. Mists of embarrassment. The rising swell and ebb of yearning.

She achieves resolution first, and with that point of purest pleasure, Mychal senses surprise and then the warmth flowing outwards as she focuses intently on the body locked so intimately with her own.

It happens sharply, almost painful, for the man, that cliff-edge and the fall and rapture. Mychal cannot experience any of this as they do; he has only the emotions that he senses, and he wonders, as he always does, what it is like to touch.

They are through now, and they settle against one another.

"Was that OK?" the man asks, as anxiety clenches again. "I wasn't too rough?"

She laughs in the continuing surprise of happiness. "Mmmm," she murmurs, her hand caressing the man's chest, and both of them laugh, as their bodies press closer.

66

And now is stillness.

The silence between them is deep and undisturbed by the sounds of traffic outside and the blurred voices from next door's TV. The silence of content. Little emanates from the two bodies now. In the aftermath of longing, its fulfilment, there is nothing further to seek, and emotions are quiet.

It is for this that Mychal conducts his vigils. It is this that assuages somehow, in a transitory way, his own loneliness and longing.

But still nothing is resolved. *It's only sex.*

Mychal sees how it might go either way. He sees how they might awake, hungover, and both tangled anew with anxieties and regret. The wrong word or clumsy gesture could undo the current closeness and she might get up and dress quickly and leave. The man might then decide, he can't do this. Better not to see her again.

But it needn't be like that. Space and time work differently for Mychal, but he can't, or won't, see the future. He sees simply how there are different possibilities.

He moves close now, spreading himself, his essence, over and through the two beings and into the minds that are drifting away from who they are and slowly towards sleep. The divide between the dimension Mychal inhabits, in which he wanders alone (if there are others of his kind he does not sense them), and theirs is not absolute. It is a spider's web, rather than rigid glass. People sometimes, he thinks, can sense him.

As he brushes his consciousness against theirs, he tries to bestow his blessing, his wish that this fleeting instant might mean more than it appears. It is here in the contentment and the flux towards sleep that people are most susceptible. Here in the barely conscious state that his presence might nudge against synapses and signals in their

67

minds, influencing, yet barely altering things, imparting knowledge, while not upsetting the fragile workings of the universe.

It is possible, he thinks, as slowly he withdraws, it is possible that on waking the man will smile at her and she'll smile back and both of them will laugh gently at the unexpectedness of this. He'll hug her close, then offer to make tea. Mychal will not return to see how she'll pull the duvet up to her chin to sip from the chipped mug, and they'll listen to the chatter of sparrows and feel the promise of the newly sun-lit day.

And perhaps they could decide: here is a beginning.

Dedication
Over the last few years, three close family members and a family friend were all diagnosed with cancer. The story is dedicated to the health care 'angels' whose good work has meant all four came through.

Over the last five years, Sarah Evans has had dozens of stories published in magazines and competition anthologies. *On such a night* was a runner up for Bridport 2008. *His Mother Tongue* won first place in the 2009 Legend Writing Award. *Afterwards* won first place in the Oct 2010 Writers' Forum monthly competition. *The Chose* appears in the 2011 Earlyworks Press anthology.

Sarah has a Diploma in Creative Writing from the Open University. She lives in Welwyn Garden City with her husband. Other interests include walking, opera and dancing.

Bad Timing

Kirsty Ferry

I already know him. It's his first day here and I search his face, wondering how I know him. I don't know his name, I don't know him personally. I just... know him. He looks straight at me, and I feel that jolt of recognition. He knows me as well. It's like our spirits recognise each other –like there's an invisible thread, holding us together. I can't explain it, but by the way he looks at me, it's as if he understands.

He's called Ed. And every night, he pops into my office and he says, "Goodnight, Kate. See you tomorrow," and he smiles at me. My name sounds special when he says it. It sounds warm, not harsh. Sometimes, he even winks at me. I smile back, and I feast on his face. I drink in the texture of his skin, the dusting of five o'clock shadow, the tiny scar beneath his left eye. His eyes are a deep, chocolate brown. They are kind, and I love them.

On my birthday he's away at a conference in Bath. My fax shrills, and I see it spewing paper out. A smile steals across my face, as a manic looking stick man appears, followed by a cake. He's drawn so many candles on it I can't count them all. Help! Help! the stick man is shouting. Call the fire brigade!

He returns the next week and pops his head into my office. I look up and see him standing there and he grins at me.

"Would you like to explain what you meant by that fax?" I cry, feigning outrage. He laughs and his eyes crinkle up at the corners. I can't help it, but my smile widens when he does that.

"I can't always be with you," he says simply. "I want

you to smile when you think of me. I smile when I think of you."

I stare at him, butterflies piling up in my stomach. Has he acknowledged it? I can hear my heart pounding and my words won't come out. Then I look him in the eyes and I finally manage to say, "Yes. I did smile. Thank you." That connection goes 'ping' between us. It shimmers and flares, just out of reach. Then it disappears. I wish I could hang on to it a little longer; hang on to him a little longer. He blushes and puts his head down. Irrelevantly, I think how odd it is to see a man blush. He turns away and makes to walk off, his head still down.

"Sorry," he mumbles. "Maybe I shouldn't have said that."

"No!" I say, too quickly. I don't want him to go. I jump out of my seat and crash around the edge of the desk. I bang my thigh on the corner of it and wince; it hurts and I know I'll be bruised tomorrow. But I don't care. I put my hand on his shoulder, holding him back. "I'm glad you said it. It means a lot to me. Thank you." I leave my hand there a little too long, and he sort of pauses. He nods. Then he looks at my leg, the one I've just banged on the desk.

"Watch yourself, Kate," he says. "You don't want to have any accidents."

Then it's my turn to blush and nod. Ed goes, and I am left in the middle of the room, wondering exactly what just happened.

After that, it becomes harder, like there are no secrets left. We can't meet each other's eyes. He stops popping into my office, and I miss him. But I still have the faxes. And the silly little emails and post-it notes he used to send me.

I realise one day that I don't know where the real Kate has gone. I'd like to find that Kate again – the Kate who danced barefoot on the beach by moonlight, and who floated naked in the ocean, counting stars and looking for comets. I think that she has dissolved like an aspirin into marriage. I wonder now, why I'd even bothered to get married. Perhaps I'd been sucked in by his easy, Irish charm. I've grown up. But does growing up mean you have to become boring and staid? My husband has remained frozen in time – ageless, preserved in alcohol like a laboratory specimen. A pickled student. He doesn't grasp the concept of marriage, mortgage or money. He laughed when I broached the subject of children.

"What the hell do you want kids for?" he'd asked, snapping the ring pull back off another can of lager. "Don't we do just fine on our own? And anyway, who would look after them? My job's not that secure so you can't give up work." He took a long drink out of the can, and burped loudly. "No," he said, shaking his head solemnly. "Best wait."

But his "secure job" never comes, and he drifts from one job to another with sickening regularity. I cringe when he comes near me. His stale breath and scratchy stubble suffocate me. I don't know if I can bring something so precious and needy into the world with that as a role model.

My telephone rings. It's my husband. And before he even tells me, I know he's walked out of yet another job.

I am still staring at the cold, soul-less telephone, when Ed comes into my office. He hovers around the door uncertainly, like a bee hovering around a plant, wondering what to do with it.

"Can I come in?" he asks quietly. I nod. He takes a step, but leaves one hand on the door handle, as if he needs support or a quick getaway.

"I've asked for a transfer," he says. Straight out. Just like that. A transfer. His face swims in and out of focus and I hear a rushing in my ears. I clutch the desk for

71

support. I can sense my world, my reason for being, imploding all around me.

"But... why?" I manage eventually. "What... what...?" How can I say, what have I done?

"I need to get away," he says. "I have to move on. And you're here. And I don't know if..." he trails off.

"You don't know what?" I whisper. My lips feel dry and parched. My hands are curled up into fists – fight or flight. Ed looks at me. His face twists as if in pain.

"I don't know how I can help you," he says. "I don't know how I can stay around you. It's complicated. Maybe I shouldn't be here. So I think it's best if I leave. I'm sorry, Kate... I..."

I shake my head.

"No – no. Don't say it. When? When do you go?"

"Monday," he replies in a low voice. "I'm so sorry."

It is Friday night, 4.30pm. I am going home to my useless, jobless husband. And Ed is leaving me in half an hour.

"Where are you going?" I have to ask. I have to know.

"Bath," he says. He looks like a schoolboy, cowed and miserable. He scuffs the toe of his shoe against the door frame. I stare at him until he raises his head and looks me in the eye. I have to be strong. "It was just... bad timing," he says softly. I nod and chew my lip.

"Yes. Bad timing. Goodbye then." I turn away. "Close the door on the way out, please."

He closes it, and it shuts with a tiny click.

I return home that night, and stand in my kitchen. I look at the pile of ironing on the table. I see the crushed, empty beer cans spilling out of the recycling box. I can hear Sky Sports blasting out from the lounge.

"Is that you Katie? What you making for tea, then?

Ah, lover, would you maybe put the kettle on while you're in there? I've had a truly terrible day, you know."

I've always hated being called Katie. Does he not realise that?

"I'm not making tea tonight," I say. "I'm sure you can do something for yourself. What else have you done today?" I can't be bothered with his attitude tonight.

"Katie, Katie, Katie!" he says, getting up out of his seat. He walks over to me, holding his arms out. In his dark, grey eyes I can just about see the man I used to love; but he's buried somewhere and I can't reach him anymore. Truth be told, I don't want to reach him anymore. I duck away from his embrace and busy myself filling the sink up with hot soapy water. I watch it swirl into the sink and feel the hot tears begin to slide down my face. Ed has gone and I'm stuck here. Why did Ed bother then? Why did he walk into my life if he was going to leave it like that? I'd sort of harboured a dream for us – a future. We'd live together happily, my husband would be non-existent… Ed was right. It was bad timing.

"I can't do this anymore," I tell the washing up. I take a swipe at the whole pile of dishes, and they clatter and splash one after the other into the sink, slopping water over the side and puddling it on the floor. I turn away from the mess and head back outside. I know I've left the water running. Well sod him, I think. He can sort it out for himself. I visualise the washing up water running steadily out of the sink and gradually filling up the tiny kitchen. The water gets deeper and deeper and obliquely I wonder whether it will start running out over the overflow when it's drowned the whole room. Then my thoughts shift and I envisage my husband floating up and away on a tide of soapy water and never having to see him again. There has to be an easier way, there has to be.

And before I know it, I am driving. I am driving too

fast and I don't have a clue where I'm going. I'm just driving. I want to be as far away as possible from my husband. If I take this motorway it will take me north. I can just keep going north and eventually I'll reach the sea. Then I might just keep on going. The other cars and the trees at the side of the road flash past me in a blur like smudged watercolours. There are lorries and vans and they are tooting their horns at me but I just keep staring at the road ahead and travelling north.

Then I think with a jolt, why the hell am I going north? Ed's south of here. He's in Bath. If I turn around, I can maybe find him. I can go to Bath and I can find him… So I see a gap in the central reservation, and before I know it, I'm heaving the steering wheel around and I'm heading to the gap so I can turn around and find Ed. The wheels are screeching on the tarmac and the engine is shuddering, trying to keep the tyres on the road. The car sort of judders along and then it slides and the toots are getting louder and there is one moment where I think Oh God, oh God, I can't keep this thing on the road; then I see a flash and I am being lifted out of my seat. Ed's face appears before me and he says, "Watch yourself, Kate. You don't want to have any accidents."

The light splinters into a thousand pieces and it's like a rainbow. I'm being lifted up on a rainbow and cushioned on a cloud. Then the world turns dark and it's silent and peaceful and I see Ed smiling at me and holding his arms out to me. So I smile back and I relax into his embrace where it's warm and safe and I can stay there forever.

After the accident, the police took me to the hospital; then I got a taxi home. I was fine. They checked me out and said it had been a minor miracle. I must have been thrown free from the car somehow. I got away with some nasty bruises, where I'd sat down hard on the grassy part of the central reservation. My husband couldn't come and collect me. He'd been too drunk to come to the hospital when they rang him. I think that was that moment where I realised I needed to make some difficult decisions.

It is Midsummer now, and I'm not that far from Stonehenge. I know that I need to be at that Summer Solstice celebration. There's nobody here to ridicule me for trying anything new and exciting. I don't think I'm as boring now – maybe the old Kate is creeping back into my life. I feel a warm glow when I think of the things she's encouraging me to do. She's definitely the one who urged me to leave the note to my husband in the fridge, sellotaped to a six pack. It seemed to be the most appropriate place.

The old Kate draws me to the Summer Solstice Celebration. I do my solstice ritual the night before – I relax and meditate over what I want from the future and what I want to give to the future. I take my rose quartz crystal, tie it into a tiny bag and set off.

I have a little one-man tent and a picnic. I park up, secure my flower garland in my hair and pad barefoot across the springy turf. The blades of grass tickle between my toes. I have never camped before, and everything is new to me. Crowds surround the monument, people of all beliefs merging into one. Young families, laughing, enjoying life, feeling free. The aroma of incense mingles with floral perfumes and sweat. Smoke curls up and away from campfires and from the tips of strange looking cigarettes. My heart lifts and I find a spot to set my things down. A small child races past me, accidentally bumping into me. The bag containing the crystal slips out of my grasp, and I swing around, trying to see where it's landed. As I bend down to retrieve it, another hand reaches it first. We stand up together, like something out of one of those corny movies. Coincidence? Or Connection? I don't know. I only know that as I stand up, our eyes lock and my heart jumps. Deep, chocolate brown eyes. Kind eyes. Eyes I had loved and still love look at me. He hands me my bag back.

"You're here," he says, smiling. I stare at him, can't stop staring. His eyes crinkle at the corners.

"I know," I say. Unconsciously, my hands curl around the hard curve of my stomach. Ed looks down and touches it gently.

"I told you to be careful, didn't I?" he says. "Not to have any accidents."

"How did you...?" I leave the words unsaid, and instead shake my head in disbelief. "I didn't even know."

"Kate, there is so much you don't know," he says to me. I feel a tiny kick inside me and look down in surprise. It's the first time. "But he knows," laughs Ed. He moves his hand to my shoulder and I feel warmth spreading through my body.

In that moment I understand some of the things Ed can't tell me. And I know I've made the right decision. I can do this on my own.

"Will I see you again?" I ask him, and he smiles at me. His eyes crinkle up again. I still love him, but all of a sudden, it's different. In the last few minutes, something has shifted.

"Some people come into your life at the right time. They are there to help you through a crisis. I was there when you needed me. I'll still be around you, but you won't always see me," he says. He leans down towards me and kisses me. I close my eyes and feel his lips gentle against mine...

When I open my eyes, he's gone. I search the crowd for him, trying to spot his familiar loping walk, his chocolate brown eyes. But he's not there. I look up to the sky and around to the monument. I think I can still feel him near me – and perhaps I always will. But I don't know whether I'll ever see him again. And perhaps that's going to be for the best. I've had enough crises; I don't want any more. I look at the bag of rose quartz in my hand and a soft glow radiates from inside it. I take the crystal out and I hold it in my palms, staring into it. I turn the crystal this way and that until I see a tiny shape inside it, a blemish on its pale pink facets. I raise the crystal up to my face, and squint at the mark.

And it looks like an angel, looking back at me.

Dedication
We all have angels in our lives. You just have to know where to look for them. My son is the closest thing I have to an angel on earth, and I'm pretty sure that my Grandma is my Guardian Angel in Heaven.

Kirsty Ferry is from the North East of England and won the English Heritage/Belsay Hall national creative writing competition (2009) and the Wyvern Publications Burning Flash Fiction Competition (2010). Her work has been published in *First Edition, Peoples Friend, Ghost Voices, The Northumbrian, The Weekly News, Wyvern Magazine,* Bridge House Publishing's *Devils, Demons and Werewolves* anthology, Wyvern Publications *Mertales* anthology and Wyvern's *Fangtales* anthology.

Finders, Keepers

A.J Kirby

I heard the car as soon as it chugged onto the street. Sounded like a tractor.

I heard the car and even before I saw it I knew it was his. Could only have been his. Quickly I climbed up from my seat, made for the front door, checked it was locked. Next in my "making like there's nobody in the house" list was to switch off the lights, and finally drawing the curtains. As my fingers gripped the faded, paisley print material I chanced a look through the gap and it was then I saw the car for the first time, and I knew for a fact it was his. The dread bubbled in my stomach. Not only did it sound like a tractor it also looked like one, as though it had been put to good use in the fields only that morning. I watched it with rapidly increasing horror as it cruised closer and closer to my house on the hunt for an elusive space.

He found one, outside Mrs. Hopkins' place (and she would have been rather less than delighted to see his car parked up in front of her place, she was very fussy at the best of times). I concentrated on wishing him away, as though by generating enough negative energy inside my house, I'd somehow force him to stay in his car, drive off again, never darken our doors. But as I watched, Carl erupted from his car and bounced down the pavement to our house like an excited puppy. In fact, describing Carl as a dog would be pretty accurate. He'd always been a bit clumsy but at the same time, he was imbued with some of that fiercely canine kind of loyalty which makes dogs so appealing to some people.

Now, I don't mean to imply that there was something

seriously wrong with Carl. He'd never been any kind of charity case and was actually of over-average intelligence. But first impressions do count. I knew for a fact that many people that I'd introduced to him simply couldn't handle his boisterous immaturity. They were repulsed by his complete lack of self-consciousness; they despised that eternal goofy grin he displayed which surely suggested that even if he wasn't entirely "gone", there was surely some loose wiring up there.

Carl lumbered up to my front doorstep. As he approached, I noticed that he was pulling this wheeled, cylindrical case, similar to a golf bag. Part of me feared that he'd perhaps packed his worldly belongings into the case and was hoping that I'd take him in as a lodger again; the other part of me wondered just what else could have been in there. Carl was always one for hare-brained schemes and it would have been just like him to turn up on my doorstep with the equipment to build a rocket in tow. He was surprisingly technologically-minded was Carl, and he knew instinctively how things worked. It wasn't beyond the realms of possibility that he could invent a rocket. Although he usually needed a good enough reason to invent something, and generally this was in order to help him find something he had (or someone else had) lost. For example, if he was to build a rocket, his reasoning behind such invention would be in order that he could discover some moon boot which the first astronauts had left behind, or one of their moon buggies. It had been the same with his up-take of archaeology – his reasoning, to discover the coins people had lost over the years, and, more recently when he'd taken up deep-sea diving for a few weeks, convinced he would find the Lost City of Atlantis. During that time, all I'd heard from him was "air-compression-tank-this" and "the-bends-that." Then, just as quickly as his ranting and raving had begun, he'd tire of his new obsession and would never mention it again.

As usual, Carl wasn't put off by the fact that the front door wasn't open and all of my curtains were shut. He must have had a sixth sense, because he never took 18 Dewar Street's initial "no" for an answer. He attacked the door as though he feared that somewhere behind it; I was maybe drowning in my bathtub or plunging my head into the oven. I tried in vain to block out the noise, wishing that some heretofore completely unheralded lightning-bolt would suddenly cut him off in mid-drum.

"Go away Carl," I whispered to myself, or to God. When Carl came a-calling, I suddenly felt closer to believing than I'd done since Primary School. The number of times I'd tried to cut deals with Him/Her over the Carl issue was staggering. So far, none of the deals had passed the proposal stage.

Hearing that the door-braying had stopped, I attempted to sneak another peek through the curtains. For about the seven-thousandth time, I was glad that he didn't have front door keys. I edged my head above the parapet – the windowsill – and gently stroked the material. I was hoping for an effect like a sudden breeze parting the curtains so as not to alert Carl to my presence, but in the end, my damn nervous twitch won out. With my typical awkward touch, I yanked the curtain half off its rail and was greeted by Carl's buffoonish face squashed up against the front window. He was looking directly at me. I knew that he knew that I'd been there all along.

I let him in. As usual, he never mentioned my strange behaviour. Without even so much as a "hello" or a "how are you," he flopped down onto the couch and launched into a madly passionate sales pitch about his new craze, which turned out to be metal detecting.

"I've been out in the fields every weekend since I got it," he said. "Got the detector off eBay – haggled 'em down to about half what he wanted at first. It's fantastic; the detector kind of cuts through the layers of time and gets you straight to the good stuff. Of course, not just anybody can do metal detecting. You have to know what you're looking for, but I got all the magazines and I've already found some Roman coins and a farmer's wedding ring. The farmer gave me two hundred quid for finding that."

As he was talking – ranting – I hardly bothered listening to the nonsense pouring from his mouth. Instead I watched as he acted out everything he said. I watched his dirty-looking dreadlocked hair spaghetti over the top of my sofa, probably leaving behind great oil-slicks. I took in full ridiculousness of Carl and his futile attempts to be fashionable; those tight black jeans which hardly held in the tree-trunk thighs of his; the deck shoes which were resting so distastefully on the edge of my coffee table; the almost see-through T-shirt.

"So how long you going to be a metal detectorist?" I asked, as soon as I could get a word in edgeways. I was still standing by my open front door, projecting about as many signs of "you are not welcome" as I possibly could. Carl, of course, did not read the signs.

"Bet you don't know the best way of searching a field for coins – the most efficient way, I mean," he said, ignoring my question.

"Get one of those archaeological underground-mapping systems that the professionals use?" I suggested, glibly.

"No, for people like me, the best way to do it is the Union Jack formation," said Carl. He folded his arms across his chest in self-satisfaction. He was a bit of a

81

fat-boy, was Carl, and when he did this, it squashed his man-boobs together to form this alarmingly high-quality cleavage. "You know how the Union Jack looks? Well, you move your detector along diagonal lines like the St. Andrew's cross..."

At some point during Carl's description of the Union Jack formation, I lost the will to live and I collapsed down onto the chair, defeated. It was only when I realised that Carl was staring directly at me, silence hanging in the air, that I understood that he'd not only stopped his diatribe, but had also most likely asked me a question.

"What was that, Carl?" I asked, making a meal of sticking my finger in my ear and waggling it around, as though I had suddenly been inflicted with a bad case of ear wax.

"I said have you heard the news about the ship?"

"The Ship?" I repeated, mindlessly. Perhaps Carl had meant my favourite pub on the sea-front. It had looked as though it was on its last legs for a while. Perhaps it had finally sunk under...

"The ship that sunk off the Bay," said Carl. "Just been on the news. Apparently, some of the freight is washing ashore now."

If Carl has the personality traits of a dog, then I'm more of a cat. I like my own personal space and am prone to bad temper when these boundaries are crossed. I sleep a lot. My loyalty, I'm afraid to say, is based on what a person can give me at that particular moment. There's still some part of myself that feels guilty for my behaviour towards Carl. I should be rewarding his commitment rather than hiding from him. The problem is, I never feel guilty enough.

Worse – part of me knew that Carl came round out of "the goodness of his heart", like he was visiting a sick relative, trying to give them something to break up the mind-numbing mundanity of the day, and I still despised him for it. I wanted nothing more than him to leave me alone for good. What possible good would it do me to trail the Seahaven beach in his wake looking for the flotsam and jetsam from the sunken vessel, The Mercury? What good would it do me, even if I happened across a beach full of priceless coins when I still felt so empty inside?

But, as I've already stated, Carl was adept at not taking no for an answer. In fact, if not taking no for an answer was a hobby, it was the one he stuck to better than any other, even train-spotting.

"We don't have to go for long; just do a St. George's cross... then we'll pop in at The Ship, have a pint," he said. One of Carl's best traps was promising a pint at the end of whatever outlandish activity he suggested. It was as though he suspected that I was such a slave to alcohol that I'd be willing to withstand two hours of humiliation just because I knew that my reward was waiting at the end. In this, as with many of his intuitions, Carl was more accurate than he probably ever knew.

"I'll just sit on the shingle and have a couple of sharpeners," I said, finally. A couple of sharpeners usually meant some of the Super Strength lager from Wagger John's Off License behind the Penny Arcade (which had long since stopped being the Penny Arcade, but was still known as that by all of the Seahaven locals. In fact, Wagger John could only have been accurately termed "Wagger" John when he was a regular absentee from Primary School; as far as I knew, he'd not missed a working day in his life, but the name had stuck.)

Carl told me more about the shipwreck on our way down to the beach. In fact, he damn near acted out the whole episode as we trotted through Seahaven's tight, winding streets. The way Carl told it, The Mercury had set out from the big docks down at Milford Haven, bound for Ireland or America. He wasn't sure which. Pretty big difference though, I thought. The ship had "got into difficulties" just as it crossed the mouth of the Bay. I wondered why nautical disasters such as this were always described so euphemistically; according to Seahaven folk, the damn Titanic probably "had a minor technical hitch".

Anyway, apparently the crossed currents at the mouth of the bay had formed some kind of whirlpool which buggered the controls, as well as some of the underside of the vessel. It had careered into the bay – usually millpond calm but in the unseasonably bad weather quite rough – and had floundered upon one of the many hidden dagger-sharp rocks which lurk under the surface.

It had taken two full days to sink. Carl was amazed that I hadn't heard anything about it, but then, as he should have known, 18 Dewar Street is not exactly top of the list for the international news-wires and, as he probably should have noticed I didn't even have a television in the house any more. When finally the waves had broken the ship, they entered, and they stole away with most of the waterlogged cargo.

"Motorbike parts," enthused Carl, although what possible use he could find for motorbike parts I dreaded to think.

"Some people are down on the beach already," he continued. "Some are wading into the sea and taking the wooden crates before they even wash up on the shore. Selling them on eBay for a fair few quid."

Another of Carl's abiding traits was his reverence for eBay. It was as though he felt that instead of faceless things like the Dow Jones and Wall Street determining the world's fiscal worth, it was instead eBay that judged how well the economy was doing, what mark-up you could put on goods and whether we are rich or poor. I envied him such naivety.

"Won't the police be making arrests?" I moaned. "I mean, this gear must belong to someone. It isn't just free-for-all just because a ship got wrecked. There is no such law as finder's keepers."

Carl looked at me as though I was the one that was naïve.

When we reached the beach, a real mob-scene had developed. Pretty much the whole of Seahaven was assembled on the shingle, shouting orders to the brave souls that were launching themselves off into the choppy water on hardly seaworthy dinghies or decrepit fishing boats. The fishing industry had long since died in Seahaven, but people seemed to have dug their old boats out of their jungle-like gardens, barely stopping to check whether there were any leaks before they charged into the sea.

A kind of madness had descended. It really was as though all of those old-fishermen's laws like "every man for himself", "finder's keepers", or "well, officer, everyone else was taking stuff, so I thought I could too," had suddenly come to pass. People who had no conceivable need for motorbike parts were piling their tractor-trailers full of the wooden crates. Even people like Mick – the town's amateur mechanic, who might actually be able or knowledgeable enough to be able to do something useful with a motorcycle part – had surely grabbed so many parts by now that he could start his own factory. Indeed, if he took many more parts, he would surely be doing himself out of a job, for soon the town's economy would become so swamped with motorbike parts that people would simply throw their bikes away, like a celebrity throws away their socks, knowing that there would always be new replacements ready to go.

A few people down by the shore recognised me and briefly nodded in my direction. They looked for longer at Carl, who was not a local and hence something of an oddity. Perhaps some suspected that he was a spy for the police, or a representative of the shipping company, although why either of those organisations would employ such a crazed-looking character was beyond me.

They looked at him even more strangely when he started to unzip the cylindrical carrying case which held his metal detector. He brought it out into the light of day like it was a light-sabre from Star Wars. And it did look quite impressive, loath as I am to admit it. It looked something like an alien's hockey-stick, if you've got a vivid imagination, or perhaps like "the vacuum cleaner of the 1990s", as imagined by one of the scientists of the 1950s on Tomorrow's World. Once Carl had assembled the shaft and head, he attached it to this back-pack which, he claimed, would generate the bleeping sound as soon as anything metallic was detected.

"Much as I don't want to point out the obvious, Carl, I'm not sure that you'll need the metal detector to locate the motorbike parts. They're all in those big wooden crates," I said, pointing out the obvious. I gestured toward the sea where another wave passed the headland, surfed by eight or nine more of the crates.

"Ah, but what if there's something more valuable on-board than just the motorbike parts?" said Carl, tapping his nose conspiratorially. He was wearing this sly grin that I didn't think I'd ever seen before. Despite my general apathy towards anything which resembled doing, seeing,

86

experiencing anything, I started to feel that my interest piqued. Indeed, that old voice in my head which spoke all of my deeply held fears and suspicions started to mutter again. It asked me why Carl had chosen today – a weekday – to pay me a visit, when usually he "popped-by" on a Saturday. Seahaven was still a trek from Cardiff, despite the high performance of his new car. There had to be something out of the ordinary to drag him here twice in a week; perhaps he knew something that the rest of the looters didn't.

Unfortunately, I had no time to quiz Carl further. Without looking back, he ran into the sea, holding his metal detector above his head as though he was afraid to get it wet; this despite the fact that he'd already told me that it was an underwater metal detector. Perhaps regardless of his surface strangeness, Carl was just like the rest of us. I remember when I bought that high-performance diving watch – apparently you could wear it up to two hundred metres underwater – and all I did was hold on to the side of the boat with my hand in the air, afraid to get the damn watch wet. But that was in long-passed times. I was not that man any more.

Past the breakers, the sea was speckled grey, like the coat of a seal pup. Carl had managed to get a fair way out by using that ungainly high-kicking running style of his and was now alongside some of the dinghies. Occasionally, a wave would send one of the crates smashing into his body, but he would just push it to one side and continue his trawl of the sea-bed. I watched him splash about, the sunlight dancing around him, forming this shimmering golden ring above his bobbing head. A religious person might have confused the reflection of the sun's rays off the water as something else – a halo perhaps. Despite everything, I gave this snort of a laugh; I could not imagine a more inappropriate angel than Carl.

I began to feel incredibly tired, then. I could see that it might be a good while before I managed to extricate him from the sea and into The Ship, and God knows how he thought he'd dry himself. The hand-dryers in there hadn't worked since about the time of the last big shipwreck in the Bay.

I slumped down onto the shingle next to the shoes and socks which Carl had so neatly arranged when he'd taken them off. I didn't even have the energy to drag myself over to Wagger John's for some cans. Even the seemingly passive act of lying down was made into an endurance test by the sharp stones of the shore and their seeming desire to roll back into the primal-soup sea from whence they came. I tried to find a way to position my body which would minimise the parts of my body which touched the shingle. I streamlined myself, as tobogganists and swimmers do. I remembered how I used to love the oldness of the stones, the possibility of fossils. I was not that boy any more.

I tried to close my eyes and think of nothing instead. I have been known to be almost Zen-like in my pursuit of thinking of absolutely nothing. Indeed, when most men get that glazed-over look in their eyes, they were probably thinking about sex, but with me, I answered truly when I said to Marie, "I'm not thinking anything." But when you're thinking about thinking nothing, you're thinking about something, aren't you? And so it was that on Seahaven beach Carl inexorably pushed me into thinking about her again. Carl was my wife's younger brother, you see. Note how I still called her "my wife", as though I still held any kind of claim over her.

Marie's family was from Glasgow. For about the first year I was seeing her, when I hadn't bothered to go up and see them, I presumed that she had a sister. This was because of her constant references to this "Car-l" (like Carol). That was how she pronounced it – a hard 'c' followed by the lilting upward slur to the rolled 'r' and almost Welsh 'l'. There was always a language barrier between us despite us both, on face value, speaking "English".

Anyway, the first time I met Carl (Carol) was when he looked after me at the wedding, when I had my episode. Afterwards, I couldn't thank him enough. To all intents and purposes, he'd saved my marriage and I just felt this overwhelming gratitude towards him; took him out with the boys for drinks on the weekend and the like. When he was kicked out of the family home, Marie couldn't have been more pleased when I made the suggestion that he come and live with us for a while down in Seahaven. Sure it was a long way away from Glasgow, but I persuaded her that it would be a good thing.

Living with Carl was about as far away from a "good thing" as you can possibly imagine. In fact, lying on the constantly shifting shingle was actually a telling analogy for how uncomfortable it was for both of us. We were only just married, in the throes of unspoiled early passion, and then there was young Carl barging in at the most inopportune moments, asking if I wanted to go fishing, or hunting for fossils, or deep-sea diving.

He always had a thing for shipwrecks when he lived with us, and I remembered his constant questions about what exactly had happened to the ships. He seemed to think that the fact that I lived by the sea was enough to make me the authority on all things nautical. I became a kind of hero to him, if it wouldn't be too big-headed to say so, because I would tell him made-up stories about how the wreck which is still there near Whitesands, for example, happened to be there. I populated my stories with landlubbers and pirates, with lost treasure and beautiful girls. I must have managed to warp the lad somehow.

After Marie left he plagued me with more questions and offers. He couldn't have been more dog-like if he'd trundled in with the lead between his teeth woofing "can we go for walkies?" But, lying on that shingle, I realised that all he was trying to do was shake me out of my crippling introspection. He wanted to wake me from that damn sleepwalking that I'd stumbled into, where all I wanted to do was lie in the dark in my room and sleep like a cat.

When I woke up, it was into that strange gloaming light along the seafront where everything seemed as though it had been painted with some thick treacle. Things moved slower. In a way, I could have been waking up into any period of my life. A sea mist had swept in and the beach was now empty. In the distance, off in the gigantic shadows cast by the rather less impressive cliffs, I could see a collection of wooden crates which looked as though they were trying to slip quietly into some of the small caves at the foot for some evening warmth.

What I noticed above all was the complete silence. It had been a long time since you could ever have termed the sea-front as lively, or noisy, but that night was eerily quiet as though the people that had flocked on the beach earlier that day were trying to put as much distance between themselves and their petty pilfering as possible. Perhaps they thought they'd found their ideal jail-bait candidate in me, asleep from all the apparent effort of moving all two hundred crates by myself.

Gingerly, I climbed to my feet. I felt as though the

whole sea had washed over me, sucking my own cargo out of me just like it had the ship. It was only when I started to walk awkwardly across the small stones that I realised that something was not right. I looked back to where I had been lying and saw one of Carl's deck shoes now looking sadly untidy without its companion arranged at right-angles to it. Carl!

Even in that first, heart-stopping moment, I knew that Carl hadn't just wandered off the beach with some new-found friends and gone to The Ship or back to 18 Dewar Street. It wasn't my discovery of the abandoned shoe that told me this. It was something much more convincing. It was that voice in my head again, telling me that Carl just wouldn't have upped and left me here, at risk of drowning.

My eyes scoured the shore for the sight of his right shoe with the rolled-up sock poking out of it like some blackened tongue. But it was too dark. Without anything but the few sad artificial lights to reflect, the water now looked like petrol. I could only just make out the white horses as the waves rolled in, more foals now.

With a sudden feeling of desperation and loss stealing over me, I started to call out for him, at first in little more than a croak but eventually in a full-throated roar. So loud were my shouts that I suspected they would start to bring people out of The Ship. People more qualified than me to mount some kind of late-night Lost at Sea search. But nobody came. For once I hated my solitude.

"Carl!" I roared again. "Are you out here, Carl?"

My voice echoed back from the cliffs.

"Carl, I'm sorry! I should have been watching!"

I should have been there for him like he'd been there for me since even before Marie and I finished. I should have been ready for something like this to have happened to him. Frantic, feeling more hopelessly alive than I'd felt

91

in I don't know how long, I stood like the French Lieutenant's Woman and I watched the sea.

I don't know how long I was watching before I realised that the thing that was repetitively banging against my leg should be investigated. Half-frozen, I inclined my head and stared down. Almost immediately, I wished that I hadn't. Being pushed against my leg by the gentle waves was the object that I least wanted to see in my whole damn life. It was the shaft of Carl's metal detector. The fabric which attached it to his backpack had frayed ends, had been sheared away by something – the sea, perhaps? I reached down and rescued the object.

As I lifted the metal detector out of the water, just like Carl himself had done, lifting it up and over my head, I saw that something was attached to it by way of a long thread which glowed, wetly, just once in the glow of one of the few lights from the pub. I started to reel in the thread, noting that although there was something attached to the other end of it, it surely wasn't heavy enough to be a body. As I reeled, I remembered making that same action a long, long time ago, when I was a boy; when I had things to live for and to look forward to.

Eventually, I saw what had been tied to the detector. It was the cylindrical canvas bag which had initially carried it. It dragged, sluggishly in the water, looking like some drowned cat. Perhaps it just wanted to sink to the depths of the ocean, just like I suspected had happened to its owner.

I yanked my catch onto the shore with a sigh of agony. What was I going to discover inside? Scarcely breathing, I unzipped the bag and reached in, part of me expecting to pull out a poisonous jellyfish, but when my hand touched something, I felt the buzz of the metal detector in my own heart. My fingers, usually so untrustworthy, closed calmly around the cold metal of Carl's sunken treasure and pulled it out of the bag. It was my own front door key. He'd had it all along.

Tears clouded my eyes. Perhaps some of the old lore still rings true; perhaps you really don't know what you'd got until it had gone. I knew then, more than anything I'd ever known in my life, that when I'd seen his bumbling form wading off into that seal-pup sea and I'd seen the sun's rays collected around his head, that it really had been a halo. Carl was my guardian angel. The front door key told me that; he could have popped in any time he'd wanted, but had allowed me to do things my own way. He'd watched over me for as long as he could though, and he wanted me to know that I'd never been alone... and I never would be.

Dedication
For Heidi, my rock, my roll, my partner, my friend, my muse, my angel

---

AJ Kirby's works have been described as modern morality tales. He is the author of four books, the dark futuristic thriller *Perfect World* (TWB Press, Colorado, US March 2011), *Mix Tape, The Collected Short Fiction*, 2007-2009, (New Generation Publishing, 2010), *Bully*, a supernatural tale of revenge from beyond the grave (Wild Wolf Publishing, 2009) and the crime-thriller *The Magpie Trap* (Youwriteon.com 2008). His short fiction has placed in numerous literary competitions and has been published widely. Andy is a reviewer for The New York Journal of Books and The Short Review, and lives in Leeds with his partner Heidi and partner in crime Eric the cat.

Fallen Angels

Sally Tarpey

Kirsten often swore when she was driving. She couldn't resist. People were such idiots, no common-sense, no consideration. Today she swore because she hadn't checked the tide timetable before she left. Getting there was the most important thing. It had to be done, she had been putting off the moment but today was the day.

The drive out of the city got better as she left the worst of the traffic behind. It was amazing how much traffic there was even before dawn. The drive to the Essex coast was quicker than expected. She wanted to be at the island causeway around sunrise.

When she got there the sun was just coming up but the road was not visible. The way was blocked by the incoming tide. She watched as a black four- by- four sent jets of water into the air. The sunlight was momentarily trapped in the droplets of water and she caught her breath at seeing the beauty of this place. A sea mist drifted in upon the tide. Wading birds gathered the last pickings along the shoreline until they too had to retreat.

Kirsten didn't really mind having to wait. She had very little time to herself at the moment and just to be able to pause and observe life was pure luxury. There was no point in trying to drive through the water and getting stuck, she decided. She looked in her rear view mirror. No one behind, so she reversed into the lay-by at the edge of the road and admired the view. Somewhere out there were the fallen angels.

The salt marshes were a favourite walking spot for her

and her mother when she was a child and the fallen angels were a favourite topic of conversation.

"What are those Mummy?" the seven year old Kirsten asked as she stood looking at the remains of the old sea defences.

"Those are the fallen angels Kirsten. They just fell out of the sky one day and the mud would not let them go. So there they have to stay."

"Why didn't they just get up and walk away?"

"The mud clings onto them. They are earthbound now. They are the protectors of the marsh. If anyone is lost when they are walking out here then the angels rise up out of the mist and guide them back to firm land. When you have found the angels then you are nearly home safe."

The story about the angels was just one of the pleasures of growing up on the island. The slight tingle of danger and adventure excited Kirsten. There were so many secret places to explore. There was the under cliff where she and her friend Marsha had made a den between the fallen tree and the cliff face. They would take it in turns to be look out. Climbing onto the tree trunk they could see up and down the beach. If anyone approached they hid and pretended they were smugglers laying in wait until their ship came to rescue them and their booty.

She must have sat for about an hour reliving the freedom of those carefree childhood days. The time before work and responsibility and her own children had pushed her sense of adventure into one small corner of her world and only let it out once a year for an annual holiday in the sun.

Kirsten noticed a stream of traffic moving past the car window, she turned on the ignition and joined it. The progress of the cars was dictated to by the ebb and flow of the sea, the passage of the moon and the turning of the earth. Kirsten liked that. It did something to redress the balance of the continuous march of man and machines upon the natural world. Sometimes she missed the feeling of being in touch with nature. The turning of the seasons didn't touch her inside her concrete cocoon. Communing with her laptop didn't give her the same energy rush. "Must do something about that before it's too late," she told the wheat fields as she passed by.

The country lane leading to the house where she was brought up had changed little over the years. The beech tree with its two main boughs outstretched still greeted her with open arms. The house had been abandoned for six months or more. *Why had she left it so long?* She didn't know what she would find, what sort of state it would be in. The neighbours had been checking on it from time to time but a house soon deteriorates once the sole living occupant has left, living human occupant that is. She fully expected the local wildlife to have moved back in. *Well, the mice had never really left.*

As the wheels of the car on the gravel drive announced her arrival she hoped that the neighbours would be out. She didn't want to be bothered with Marsha. Her constant chatter was fun when they were children but now... *You can't pretend you've got cut off when the person is standing right in front of you can you?*

Kirstin moved quickly from the car to the house without using the remote locking so as not to further alert anyone who might be listening. The musty smell hit her at once and she moved through to the kitchen to open the back door. The pile of mail neatly stacked on the hall table indicated that Marsha must be checking the house on a regular basis. At least that was one thing she needn't worry about. All was tidy in the kitchen. She checked the pot plants and they needed a little water but otherwise everything was in order. She gathered a few bin liners and plastic carrier bags from the cupboard under the sink.

Start in the bedroom then and work my way down. Kirsten opened her mother's bedroom door carefully as if she might disturb a still sleeping figure in the bed. Strange how she still expected to see her lying there. She set to with energy, if not enthusiasm, for the task. She opened the wardrobe door and threw armfuls of clothes still on their hangers on the bed. She pulled the suitcases out from under the bed and emptied the contents of the tights and sock drawer into one of the bags. Uneasiness washed over her about handling her mother's things without her permission. Some instinct made her turn to see if she was being watched but all she caught was her own reflection in the full length mirror. She grabbed a pink and purple floral dress from the pile on the bed and threw it over the glass.

If you cover the mirror then the evil spirits cannot find you. She surprised herself at this thought. *Where had that ridiculous idea come from?* She was a professional woman with a logical mind, not some naive believer in superstition and witchcraft. All the same she let it lie. The piles of clothes on the bed grew and grew. Kirsten decided that very few of them were wearable, not even suitable for the charity shop; they joined the bags of shoes and underwear on the first leg of their journey to the tip. One person's life consigned to a collection of carrier bags.

She looked around the room. It was a mess. Her mother would have a fit. The dressing table with the engraved silver hairbrush, mirror and comb lay neatly on the lace edged runner like an accusation of Kirstin's guilt. She was responsible for the events of the past half year and now she was responsible for this violation of her mother's room. The job seemed interminable and she tired of the

97

constant banging in her head caused by forcing all the emotions back inside until they had nowhere else to go.

She felt the howl begin deep inside her brain. It moved to her eyes but the tear ducts were not the way out. It moved to her ears where the thrum of silence beat it back. Then it found its escape route. Kirstin threw back her head, her mouth dropped open and she howled. She howled so loudly and uncontrollably she wondered where the noise was coming from. She moved back to the mirror and pulled away the dress. She looked at the face in the mirror but the face looking back at her was not hers – it was her mother's.

"Come with me Kirstin. I want to show you something." Kirstin followed the voice in her head. She went silently down the stairs, through the hallway, into the kitchen and out through the back door to the shed at the bottom of the garden. The wooden shed was almost falling down. Kirstin had not been in it for years. Whenever she came back home she always offered to help her mother sort it out, along with the other clutter- filled spaces in the rambling Victorian house. They had tackled the loft and the cellar from time to time but the spaces always got filled up again, in the same way that the rain butts collected water. But the shed, the shed was always the next job to be done and consequently it never was.

"It's a bit late for the grand sort out now don't you think?" said Kirsten. "We could just put a match under it I suppose."

She opened the door and shifted the old petrol lawn mower out of the way so that she could at least reach the boxes and old suitcases that lined the walls. She opened one cardboard box and pulled out a newspaper dated 1964. It was from the Daily Recorder, the local paper that no longer existed. Her mother's explanation was that it had,

"Outlived its usefulness. A bit like me I suppose." Kirsten had disregarded that statement at the time but now she could feel the force of its impact between her ribs. She had convinced herself that she had done all she could to leave her mother in the independent life style she so loved. She had to move to London, the work was there and the commute was getting too much for her. She was not seeing enough of her children and her marriage was suffering too. Miriam's refusal to come with them was a constant irritation and a worry. But it was her choice to stay. Kirsten made regular phone calls and visited at least once a month but Miriam didn't even try to understand the pressures on Kirsten.

"Don't know where this drive to live in the city comes from? You have always been a country girl at heart. London is no place to bring up children. Sooner or later you will end up collecting them from casualty or the police cells. Is Stephen in agreement with your decision?"

"It's not my decision it's our decision Mum. It's the only practical way out. We both work in town. Our family is falling apart Mum."

Once the move had taken place Kirsten's relationship with Miriam changed. Visits turned into a list of jobs for Kirsten to do and the stack of whiskey bottles for the bottle bank continued to grow. Kirsten tried to persuade Miriam to move into a smaller place and showed her brochures about warden assisted flats but they always ended up in the bin. When Kirsten arrived one weekend last January to find Miriam in a semi-comatose state, sitting in an armchair with layers of blankets and coats on top of her because she forgot how to put the heating on, the decision was taken out of Miriam's hands. She had not been in a fit state to put up any resistance when the ambulance arrived. Miriam survived the hypothermia and it looked as though she intended to survive the continuous pressure from family, neighbours and friends to be "looked after" but in the end she had no choice. *Just like I had no choice but to find her a place in a care home, thought Kirsten.*

Kirsten couldn't think about it anymore. She must get on with what she had come here to do. Whatever had diverted her from the tasks in the house now guided her attention to the first box. Each item had been carefully wrapped in newspaper to protect it from the ravages of time. Objects made of porcelain and glass and cosseted from daily use did not show the passage of the years, unlike the sculpted faces of the sick and old. She remembered the commemorative tea pot stand from the Coronation that was kept in the glass display cabinet and only came out at Christmas time. Most of the items in the box belonged to her grandparents and she could even recall where each one used to be kept in their meticulous house. *Pity tidiness wasn't a family trait they passed on.*

"You just left it all for years and years Mum. Emptied their house and then couldn't bring your-self to throw the memories away. Well I'm not falling into that trap."

"Hello, anyone at home? Hello Kirsten is that you?"

The voice from the garden belonged to Marsha, her childhood friend who had stayed living in the village long after other school friends had departed for other lives. Kirsten cursed herself for speaking her thoughts out loud. If she had kept quiet she might have been able to avoid showing herself. Marsha must have heard her.

"In here Marsha."

"Oh my, what a heap! Such a lot to do Kirsten. Do you want some help?"

Not really, thought Kirsten but what came out of her

100

mouth was, "Okay, yes thanks Marsha. Could you get some black bin bags from the kitchen for me please? They're in the cupboard under the sink, huge roll of them."

"Guess you're going to need a huge roll if every room is like this shed. Bit of a hoarder Miriam was."

"Don't talk about her in the past tense Marsha. She's not dead yet, just not well enough to run this house anymore."

"Sorry, yes, clumsy of me. Black bin bags then, won't be long."

Kirsten went back to her investigation of what was inside the various bags and boxes. Each one held items that had not been on a shelf or in a cupboard for years. So why keep them? She despaired of getting any semblance of order in this chaos. She sneezed three times as the accumulation of disturbed dust in the air began to get to her.

Marsha returned with the roll of bags. "Phone went while I was in the house," she said, "so I answered it. It was Stephen wanting to know if you got here ok. He said your mobile was switched off and to switch it on, he will call you later."

"Bugger," Kirsten mumbled.

"Have you thought about doing a car boot?" Marsha said," I did one last week and made forty pounds. It's amazing what people will buy."

There was something Kirsten found slightly uncomfortable about the idea. These things were important to her mother. She didn't want strangers turning them over and haggling about what they were worth.

"Maybe," Kirsten said. "Could you just give me a hand with pulling that chest of drawers away from the wall please Marsha?"

They hauled together and slowly the mahogany chest inched its way until it no longer stood with its back to the world but displayed three deep drawers. Kirsten pulled out the first drawer. There were crayons and paints and pencil cases, rulers, staplers and scissors, tubes of glue (dried up long ago) and sheets of coloured paper and shapes for drawing round. Kirsten was immediately transported back to the time when she loved to make things. She spent hours sticking and painting and drawing. Hers was a very happy childhood, creating things. No wonder she ended up being a designer.

"What do you want done with this lot?" Marsha asked.

"Well do you know any children who might want the pencil crayons? I hate throwing this sort of stuff away. There are too many children in the world who don't have enough writing and drawing materials."

"Oh I agree but how are you going to get it to them Kirsten? I don't think Parcel Force go to Malawi or Haiti."

"Ditch it all then."

Marsha held open the bag while Kirsten dumped the contents of the drawer.

"It can all go. No hesitating, just get shot of it all. Would you mind taking this lot out to the car for me please Marsha?"

The notebook was right at the bottom of the second drawer. Kirsten almost missed it. She nearly tossed it into the consignment for the landfill along with all the old newspapers, magazines and piles of yellowing paperwork. It was a very ordinary, grey, spiral bound notebook but what captured Kirsten's attention was the fine pencil drawing of an angel on the front cover. Kirsten noted that the drawing was very detailed and carefully done. She opened it and started reading.

She recognised her mother's handwriting and immediately felt as if she was reading a private diary, thoughts meant for her mother's eyes only. *But the opening sentence was addressed to her. She was meant to have it – just not now.* She looked towards the door of the shed, like a furtive child, fearful of discovery doing something she ought not to be doing. *Marsha would be back any minute.* She needed time and solitude not the prattling Marsha. *How to get rid of her?*

"Sorry Marsha. Got to go, Stephen called me again. I need to go home right away."

"Children all right?"

"Oh yes, work related stuff. You know how it is?"

"Oh yes I know how it is."

As Kirsten moved out of the shed and across the garden to the car Marsha trailed after her with the second black bag.

They loaded the second bag into the car. Marsha noticed the book in Kirsten's hands.

"Saving that one?"

"Oh that! Yes just an old school book of mine, sentimental value. Must run, thanks for your help Marsha. See you next weekend perhaps."

When she had cleared the outskirts of the village she pulled the car into a farm track and opened the book to read on:

I wouldn't say I was a religious person Kirsten but the day I knew I was pregnant with you I felt I had been kissed by an angel. Conceiving you was not the easiest thing in the world. My prime fertility was at a time when in-vitro fertilisation was not even thought of. Your father and I desperately wanted children but month after month I looked for the signs of pregnancy and I was always disappointed. Forgive me for not telling you this sooner but I could not find the words. Somehow the time was never right. When you were old enough to understand about love and sex and the whole relationships mine field you were too busy trying to come to grips with your own sexuality to be interested in mine.

Then when you married Stephen and you walked down the aisle of our parish church on your father's arm I saw the pride in his eyes and the joy in yours. I could not tell you then.

The birth of your first child seemed a missed opportunity and I resolved to tell you when you said you were pregnant for the second time. I weakened again. Surprising, you might think, for an outspoken and forthright woman like me.

So the time for angels is now. Do you remember when we went walking on the marshes and you asked me about the dark shapes in the mist? I told you they were fallen angels. This is why.

It was on that spot that you were conceived. I had been walking with your uncle Keith. Your father was away on a conference. He was often away for long periods of time, working. His brother Keith dropped by sometimes to keep me company. We got along very well together. In fact if I had not married your father I would have married him. He asked me to go away with him when we were younger but I was already courting your father. We didn't do that sort of thing in those days, two timing it was called. I won't say I wasn't attracted to him, Kirsten, because I was and that's the truth of it.

It all happened very quickly. We sat down to rest. We had been walking for hours. He took off his jacket for me to sit on. As he touched me I felt that I was observing what was happening between us from a distance and was powerless to control it. After we had made love I should have felt remorse at the betrayal of your father but I didn't. My first thought was that if I became pregnant the baby would look exactly like my husband (your father and his brother were so alike). I actually prayed that I would conceive. My prayers were answered Kirsten. You will always be my angel but of course sometimes even angels fall.

I will not know how this news will be received by you but my hope is that you will forgive me the years of deception. Think of the fallen angels and how they can guide lost souls out of the mist. Think of a barren life as compared to the joy of a family. Your father forgave me. Perhaps you will too.

Kirsten placed the book on the passenger seat and started the car. She drove in a hypnotic state not knowing what to feel. How could her mother keep such a secret for so long? She must try to talk to her.

As she entered the room she saw her mother sitting in her usual spot in her armchair by the window. "Blasted squirrels have been at the bird table again," Miriam said without even looking up, "Bring me a shotgun and I'll shoot the little vermin. You know where father keeps his gun. In the cabinet on the left as you go down the hallway."

"Hello Mum," Kirsten said disregarding the rant that was her mother's current favourite replay. *Good sign, thought Kirsten. If she's complaining that means she's having a good day. I might get some answers.*

Miriam turned her head and said, "What's that book you have there?"

"It's yours. I found it while I was clearing out the shed. Do you recognise it?"

Kirsten placed the book in her mother's lap. Miriam's fingers delicately traced the outline of the angel and the corner of her mouth twitched.

"In the shed?"

"Yes Mum, I thought you might be able to tell me about it. How long it's been there, when you were going to give it to me. You drew this picture of an angel. Do you remember Mum? Please tell me you remember. I can't do this on my own."

"Is it time for our drawing class? Are you the new teacher? I like drawing. I'm good at it."

"This is your writing too. How long ago did you write this Mum?"

"Oh it's the writing class is it? Are you the new teacher? I'm good at writing. I used to write poetry. Had some published you know."

"That's right Mum, you did. You wrote poems and they were published in a women's magazine. Do you remember when you wrote this?"

Miriam turned the pages of the notebook. Her expressionless face gave away nothing. Her eyes registered nothing. She wasn't even focusing on the page but gazing out of the window.

"Why didn't you tell me Mum? If Dad knew too why didn't you both tell me? You may be suffering from dementia Miriam but you have to remember writing this. I'm not taking responsibility for this too. I'm not telling Keith that I'm his daughter – that's your responsibility."

Kirsten grabbed Miriam's shoulders and began shaking her. "You must remember. This is about you and Keith. You have to tell him before it's too late. Don't leave this up to me Mum."

One of the nurses persuaded Kirsten to let go of her mother and took her along to the kitchen for some tea. She tried to explain that Miriam's memory loss was extreme. She might never regain certain memories and others she would keep repeating like a bad weather forecast.

Kirsten left without saying goodbye to her mother. *What was the point? She didn't know I had arrived so she won't care that I have gone. Perhaps that's how I should cope with this? If it stays unspoken then no-one will know or care, no one except me.*

She drove back to the causeway, parked the car in the lay-by and walked out across the marsh to find the angels. She slipped the notebook into her jacket pocket. At first she kept to the paths and then thought *to hell with it. I'm going creek hopping.* She cleared the first two creeks easily. The spongy marsh plants absorbed her weight and formed a carpet landing. She was getting muddy and spoiling her new beige leather shoes and cream trousers but she didn't care.

The third creek was wider and she hesitated just long enough to lose the momentum. She completely misjudged it and her foot slipped on the salt water soaked purslane fringing the edge of the creek. She tumbled down and a pain shot through her wrist as she grabbed the plants in an attempt to stop herself from falling into the water. She cried out as she hit the surface of the murky sludge. She was soaked through and her legs were firmly embedded in the glutinous mud. She was held fast. She reached for the bank. Every time she tried to take her weight on her arms and drag herself up her wrist gave out and the pain forced her to stop. She listened. A gentle lapping sound and the screech of a lone curlew pierced the silence. She could see the evening sun beginning to fall, leaving streaks of red and orange and purple, silken threads drawing together, merging sea and sky into one. Soon all the colours of the ending day would combine, leaching the contrasts from the landscape, a palette of greys. She felt no sense of panic but a kind of absence of all feeling. She stopped struggling and reached inside her jacket pocket. The notebook was wet but still readable.

She lay still, leaning against the bank and waited. A gentle sound moved in rhythm to the water and the wind. *Must be the fallen angels, they sing so sweetly. They must be close because I can feel them. No need to search any more. I can see the way home.*

Kirsten used her good arm to dig a hole in the side of the bank between the tangled salt water plants, the sea lavender and glasswort. She took one last look at the angels and pushed the book inside the hole, into the dark. *Some things were never meant to leave the place that gave them life, the place where the past, the present and the future become one. They were destined to remain buried.* "Go and join them," she said" Go and join the earthbound ones. You belong here. I have brought you home."

Dedication
In memory of Lewis whose strength and endurance is an inspiration to us all

---

Sally is a retired teacher who has always been hooked on storytelling. She began writing short stories for children whilst working as an education volunteer in Cambodia and hasn't stopped travelling and writing since. She is currently writing short stories for adults, studying creative writing with the Open University and drafting the opening to a novel.

On Angels' Wings

Misha Herwin

"It's time to go home." Sister Frances stood in the doorway of the art room, a study in black and white under the harsh neon light. Gillian, head bent over the table, lank hair falling over her face did not look up.

"Five o'clock. Sister Patrick will be locking the gates," the nun continued. Gillian's shoulders tensed. Charcoal clenched in her fist she hunched over her work shading furiously. Then lifting the sheet to the light, she studied it intently.

"It's no good," she said at last.

"I don't agree." The nun glided towards her. "You are too hard on yourself. All it needs is a touch, here, a touch there." She stretched out her hand to demonstrate.

"It's rubbish." With a savage gesture Gillian ripped the drawing from top to bottom. Then snatching up the two halves she tore at them until drifts of paper lay around her feet like dirty snowflakes.

"Was that really necessary?" Sister Frances said. "Your portfolio is hardly full and the closing date for the scholarship is in two weeks time. You have every chance of getting into the art school but you have to have something to show the selection panel. You understand how important this is, don't you?"

"Yes," Gillian snarled, then clapped her hand over her mouth as she saw the startled expression on the nun's face. At St Catherine's no girl was ever rude to the nuns. "Sorry," she muttered. "But it's no good. I can't do it. It was all in my head, but I couldn't get it down and now." She kicked the scattered scraps of paper towards the bin. "It's all pointless."

"No," Sister Frances said softly, her face pale and

bland as a communion wafer. "You need to think. To reflect on what you have done and how you could improve…" the rest of her sentence was drowned out by the slam of the art room door.

Eyes sharp with tears, footsteps echoing eerily through the deserted corridors, Gillian blundered past empty classrooms, down the great oak staircase, forbidden to all but the teachers and senior perfects and out into the gloom of the tree shaded drive.

She'd fought so hard to be here. Her parents had made it plain that they weren't going to support her through college. The headmistress didn't want her in the sixth form and if it hadn't been for Sister Frances begging for a second chance she'd have had to get a job like her sisters. Still she had hung on. Sister Frances had found the scholarship, helped her fill in the forms, plan the projects for her portfolio and now, after all that, she wasn't going anywhere.

"Was it the detention again?" Sister Patrick asked as she locked the gates behind her, but Gillian's throat was tight, her teeth clamped into her lower lip and she could not reply. Her feet slipped on the damp pavement, her breath came in short sharp sobs as she climbed the hill to the main road. Going left would take her past the lighted windows of the shops to the bus stop, where the final gaggle of maroon uniformed girls would be crowding into the shelter. At this time of day they would be either members of the school hockey team coming back from practice, or the goody-goody girls, the ones who joined clubs or stayed behind for extra study. They were pathetic, all of them. They'd stand there giggling and gossiping and give her that look. That pious self satisfied, half pitying glance they bestowed on anyone who broke the rules and got themselves into trouble with the nuns.

Well she wasn't going to explain and she wouldn't

give them the satisfaction of thinking they were right, again.

She had no friends at St Catherine's. The other girls only pretended to like her. When they found she didn't have a big house and a car they dropped her. But she didn't care. She didn't want to be friends with them anyway.

Heaving her bag more firmly on her shoulder, Gillian set off in the opposite direction. To get to the next bus stop her way ran through the old cemetery. Once past the two empty plinths, which marked the entrance to the graveyard, her breathing slowed. Ancient yews masked the harsh glow of the street lamps and no one could see her in their comforting darkness. No one cared who she was, or what she was doing. Her hands unclenched, her limbs loosened. Here she was safe, here she could think.

Slowly she walked past crumbling headstones and broken crosses until she came to a row of elaborate mausoleums. There were temples and chapels, domes and towers their once bright marble pitted and stained. Further on there were simpler tombs, flat topped, speckled with lichens, yellow and brown as an old man's skin, or furred with a sinister green slime. Choosing one of these Gillian dropped her bag on the worn relief of a skull and curling her arms around her knees sat staring into the gloom.

What was she going to do? More than anything else in the whole world she'd wanted to go to art college and now she'd ruined her chances. No. That wasn't true. She straightened up and glared into the twilight. She hadn't ruined anything it was just that she was no good. Sister Frances was wrong about her. She couldn't draw, she couldn't paint. She couldn't do anything. She was useless.

"She only did it to stop me getting into trouble," Gillian muttered. And even that hadn't worked. When she was in the art room, she behaved, kept her head down, got on

111

with her work. The rest of the time, she was a teacher's worst nightmare. She was always late, she couldn't keep her mouth shut, never got her homework in on time, came bottom in tests. But it didn't matter. Nothing mattered. Not anymore. Gillian twisted a strand of hair around her finger and tugged viciously.

She was going to have to do it. She was going to have to say it. Her mum and dad were right and she was wrong. From the start when she told them she wanted to be an artist when she grew up, they'd told her she'd better think again. Art didn't get you a good job. She'd be better off working at Wills the tobacco factory. There was good money to be made, a secure job to be had for life, as many free fags as you could smoke and she could start as soon as she left school at sixteen. What more did she want for goodness sake? But no she wouldn't listen. She thought she knew better.

She'd not learned anything useful at St Catherine's like typing or cooking. The nuns had always gone on about her God given talents and the opportunities she'd been given because she was brighter than so many other poor girls. Well, she'd thrown away her chances. The best she could hope for was that she'd be allowed to go to the poly to do a secretarial course.

As for God, if He really cared about her, like the nuns said He did, then He wouldn't have let this happen. Gillian scraped her nails along the surface of the stone, until she'd gouged out two white lines and her hands were green and blackened with slime. Then she slid from the tomb, wiped her palms on her skirt and reached for her bag. There was no point in waiting any longer, she might as well go and get it over with.

Her dad would be all right. He'd put his arm around her shoulders and tell her it didn't matter, she was still his little girl but her mum, she'd be so pleased at the way it had all turned out. She'd never liked having a daughter at the grammar school. Still if she wasn't home soon, her mum would start to worry and when she got in she'd get a right telling off.

Head bent, shoes scuffing at the cracked flagstones, she missed the strand of ivy snaking across her path. Twisting around her ankle it threw her off balance. Throwing out her arms to save herself she staggered to a halt against a pillar. Gasping for breath she clasped cold stone. Her bag slid from her shoulder and hung heavily from her wrist. It banged against her side and she pushed herself upright. As she did so, her fingers closed around a carving of a girl's head. Done in relief, it showed a shapely profile, a slightly tipped up nose, hair bound back by ribbons in the Grecian style with wisps and curls escaping to soften the outline of her face. Below it words eaten away by the years was the inscription.

"Anne-Marie, beloved daughter died in her eighteenth year. Granted the vision of eternity."

Above the crumbling letters, rose the statue of an angel. Wings outstretched as if protecting the girl lying beneath, it was chipped and battered. The tip of a wing was missing and the fingers of one hand had gone, while the other hung loosely, its metal rod eroded by rust.

"It's not fair." Gillian screwed up her eyes, uncertain whether the tears that suddenly blurred her vision were for herself or the girl that had died so long ago. The damp cold seeped through her thin coat. She shivered and rubbed her sleeve across her face. A chill breeze sprung up, ruffling the hairs at the back of her neck, then dying down as quickly as it had come. But in the still silent air, the feathers of the angel's wing fluttered, its head bowed and an expression like a smile passed over the weather worn face.

Was it a trick of the light? The far off beam of a car turning the corner? Her imagination? Whatever it was the cold misery that had almost paralysed her lifted. Warmth flowed back into her limbs and she rummaged frantically in her bag. She knew she was never going to draw again, she knew that part of her life was over, but she couldn't stop. Pulling out her sketchbook, she propped it against her waist and began.

Peering through the dimness wasn't easy, her lines were hard, black, swift. In a few quick moments it was done. Anne-Marie's face framed by the suggestion of an angel's wing. Chewing her lip, she examined it critically. It was too one dimensional, too flat and what was worse a load of sentimental rubbish. What was she thinking of? No angel had looked after this girl. If it had she wouldn't be lying here so young. No one had cared, let alone some stupid spirit in a white dress that was supposed to watch over you all the time. Whatever the nuns said they didn't exist. Who could possibly believe in something that never left your side, not even when you were on the toilet? That was just mad. Angels were rubbish, just another thing nuns made up to keep you good. She should never have let this one into her picture.

Ripped from the page, the drawing drifted slowly to the ground, finally snagging on a piece of broken wing. It hung like a moulted feather, black and white against mottled marble, its flatness emphasising the three dimensional solidity of the sculpture. Solid yet ethereal. It promised flight, hope, rising up out of this world. Moving on to something better. Maybe it hadn't all ended here.

As Gillian stooped to pick up her drawing something brushed against her cheek. Soft as fingers against her face, then it was gone. She knelt down and ran her hands over the long cool sweep of the wing. She knew now what she

114

had to do. No one would miss it. No one would even know it was gone. Besides, she needed it. She had to have it. She glanced over her shoulder. No one. She listened. Only the faint hum of the traffic far below at the bottom of the hill. Grinning, she stretched up and standing on the tips of her toes caught hold of the angel's hand. Another glance just to make sure. Then a quick wrench. A shower of rust descended on her head followed by a sharp snap as the hand came away. Hurriedly she stowed it in her bag, followed by the piece of wing.

Next morning the air was crisp with a hint of frost. Gillian caught the early bus got off at the cemetery stop and walked slowly through the graveyard, searching and gathering. From time to time she stopped to cut a few sprigs of yew, a spray of scarlet berries, to kneel at the side of a tomb and rub the lichens and mosses onto the pages of her sketchbook.

The school gates were open, but the doors locked. There had to be a way in. She couldn't wait to start. Clutching her bag Gillian slipped round the side of the convent, scuttled down the stairs towards the temporary building the girls used as a dinner hall. If she was right, the cooks sometimes left one of the side doors ajar.

"Please God," she prayed as she skirted the corrugated iron walls. "Thank you," she breathed as the handle gave at her touch and she stepped inside.

The light in the art room was clear and cold sharpening every detail. Gillian took what she'd gathered out of her bag and began.

"What are you doing here?" Sister Frances arrived obviously alerted by the duty nun. "You should be in the hall," her voice died away, her hands flying to her mouth as she saw what Gillian was doing. "What is it?"

"I don't know." Gillian was alight. "I just know it works."

"I've never seen anything like it." The nun stepped back gazing at the work. Beneath the shadow of the broken wing, the assembled pieces showed sadness and tragedy, the shortness of life thrown into greater contrast by the vibrancy of a young girl's face. The symbols of death, the yew and its berries were paradoxically both the blood of sacrifice and the blood of life. Reference pages torn out of a history book put Anne-Marie into context. Black ribbon hung with silver stars symbolised the fullness of her life however brief. In the palm of the angel's hand Gillian had placed her own photo. She was wearing a mini skirt and her eyes were lined with heavy black makeup.

Sister Frances shook her head.

"I'm lost for words," she said finally. "It's not drawing, it's not sculpture, it's not quite collage. To be frank I don't know what to call it but it is a very powerful piece."

"I know," Gillian said simply. "It's me and I'm calling it 'On Angels' Wings'."

Dedication
This story is for Wendy, Guy and all the other angels in my life

---

As a writer for both children and adults Misha is fascinated by the supernatural and the uncanny. In her career she has published three books for children: *Dragonfire, Juggler of Shapes* and *Master of Trades*. Besides books she also writes plays, which have been performed by Theatre in Education companies and short stories for adults and children, some are in anthologies, some have been broadcast on radio. She also runs workshops in schools and museums.

http://misha-herwin-writer.blogspot.com

Quarterly Evaluation

Raphaela Bruckdorfer

Nathaniel looked at the piece of paper in front of him on the desk. "QUARTERLY EVALUATION" it read.

"This is the Evaluation of the month JANUARY. Its purpose is to improve your working conditions, as well as to gain some insight into our employees' assessment of our company. Please note that all the gathered information is treated with strict confidence. Even though this Evaluation is not anonymous, we would like to emphasize that AT NO POINT will it have any influence on your yearly staff report. Nevertheless, we take for granted your absolute honesty. Remember: the analysis of the collected data is of use to every part of our team, so answering the following questions sincerely should lie in your own interest."

He had closed his eyes and had recited this passage from memory. Having worked in this place for longer than anyone could remember, he knew it by heart.

"Okay, let's get this done..." Nathaniel said to himself.

Name? This one was easy. In his neat, elegant handwriting, he printed *"Nathaniel"* on the sheet.

Momentary department? Finding the answer to that one didn't really require lots of brains either. "Child safety and protection," he wrote.

"Duration of employment?"

"Let me think... When was my promotion? Was it six or seven years ago? I can't recall. Well, I'll get back to it later..." he mumbled. *"When was your last wing-inspection?* My last wing-inspection? Good question!

March, I think. Yeah, it was sometime around Easter. So, let's write March."

Without his noticing, his tongue had wandered out between his lips and into the right corner of his mouth. He did that whenever he concentrated on something really hard.

"M-A-R-C-H," he spelled. "March." Satisfied, he glanced down.

"When was your halo's radiance last measured? Oh Lord…"

"YES?" a deep, vibrant voice interrupted his thoughts.

"I am sorry, My Lord, I was just thinking out loud," Nathaniel squeaked sheepishly, his cheeks burning with embarrassment.

"THIS HAS BEEN THE FIFTH TIME THIS WEEK!"

"I know, I know! I'm *really* sorry, My Lord! It's just that I can't get used to this new rule."

"LET US BE GRACIOUS AND FORGET ABOUT THE INCIDENT. TIME WILL TEACH YOU, I HOPE."

"Of course it will, Your Highness! Again, I can only utter my most sincere apologies for having caused You troubles. I will try everything to keep to the new Rule 289 405."

"YOU MAY."

As suddenly as the voice had appeared it had vanished again and left Nathaniel alone with his paper.

"These stupid rules! Who needs a rule that tells you not to use all The Lord's" – "NATHANIEL!!!"

"I'm sorry, I am sorry!" The angel ducked down, throwing frightened glances over his head. "Who needs a rule that tells you not to use all *His* equivalent names unless speaking to Him personally? I'm not the youngest anymore; my memory won't improve with the years!" He almost cried with anger now. "All right... I guess it's of no use feeling sorry for myself. Today's just not my day... How I *hate* filling out these questionnaires... What's up next? *Are you satisfied with your employment*? Am I satisfied? I don't know... Yeah. It's not so bad, I think. At least it's much better than it was in the Christmas-letter-department. Boy, this was *nasty*! Flying around in the cold and dark, collecting paper from window sills, always trying not to crash into the glass... How glad I am to be able to call this the past! And then – in summer I had to help out everywhere they needed someone, being every-body's punching bag... No! I don't even want to *think* about it! So, yes, I *am* satisfied... *Do you feel comfortable in your working environment (the before-used term "environment" refers to colleagues, equipment and surroundings)*? *Absolutely*! The guys I'm in a team with are *great*! Afriel's *so* funny! Always makes everyone crack up with laughter! And Sablo – our "clever-one"... Okay, *colleagues* done. Equipment and surroundings are acceptable, I'd say." Nathaniel jotted his opinion down.

"*Is there anything you especially like about your job*? You bet!" Eagerly, he wrote: "I love it when children, who have involuntarily and without their own notice endan-gered their precious lives, thank me for having saved and protected them." The angel paused for a moment, then muttered: "This sounds as if *all* of them were grateful! Chance would be a fine thing! Some of them are such unappreciative, spoiled little brats! Shout at me: how *dare* you, scaring me like that?" he mocked. "What do they think?! I haven't stolen my time either! There are lots of things I'd rather do than jump into an icy lake to pull them out when they've broken in, or hopping onto a hot stove so they don't burn their lovely, tender fingers... Ha! As if I actually had a *choice*! My contract is binding; even if I

119

wanted to see them drown or burning (which I do *not*, of course) I couldn't *let* them, for I had to swear a holy oath..."

Nathaniel jumped almost a metre high, when all of a sudden a loud, irritating "*BEEP, BEEP, BEEP*" was heard out of his bag.

"Not *again!*" the angel moaned. "Can't I even fill out this stupid questionnaire without being interrupted?!"

He longed into the linen thing and produced his beeper. He dialled the number he saw on the display.

Immediately, a female voice answered: "You are wanted at Times Square *right now!*"

"The case?" Nat asked for further information.

"Car accident," the female retorted.

"'Kay. I'll be there in no time."

Almost before he finished his last sentence, Nathaniel found himself on the busy street. He turned his head sharp left and correctly assessed the situation.

Only a second later, brakes squealed, people screamed and the angel lay on the bonnet of a yellow car.

Behind him on the zebra crossing stood a boy – he couldn't be older than seven or eight – staring at the white-clothed "man" in bewilderment. He pulled the earplugs of his iPod out of his ears. "What are you *doing* there?" the little fellow enquired in puzzlement.

"Well, what does it *look* like, little sport, huh? Probably saving your *life?*"

Nathaniel stood up and was dusting his "outfit", even though this was rather for creating an impression on the almost-run-over-by-a-car-kid than for means of requirement.

"*Why?*" The boy suspiciously narrowed his eyes.

At this point, Nathaniel would have enjoyed to give

120

his anger about people's inattention and risky behaviour free reign; still, he kept it to himself. Firstly, he wasn't allowed to intentionally expose himself as what he was – a God sent creature; and secondly, he thought it better to calm the boy. The little fellow only now had become aware of the disaster he had escaped by a hair's breath.

"Because this guy," – Nat pointed accusingly at the sturdy lad who had got out of his automobile – "or rather his *vehicle*, would have mashed your fragile body if I hadn't intervened and thrown myself in front of it."

"*Oh.*" The youngster raised his hands, looked at them as if to check whether his fingers were all where they belonged, and stared hard at the unexpected saviour. "Thank you!" he wanted to say; yet, the declaration never left his mouth. Obviously, he was totally lost for words.

Nevertheless, Nathaniel comprehended his gratefulness and nodded politely. "To actually say it has been my *pleasure* would be a lie, but, yeah, you're welcome."

He smiled his special, genuine angel-smile.

"*OH MY GOD! ARE YOU ALLRIGHT?*" The car driver had placed his enormous paws on the charge's shoulders and was shaking him.

"Let *go!*" the eight-year-old squeaked and stepped back.

"I'm sorry! Gosh, I'm *so* sorry!" The man cried with shock.

"You would have mashed my fragile body if this strange man in that weird white nightshirt hadn't intervened and thrown himself in front of your *vehicle!*" the nipper echoed reproachfully.

Whether it was the boy's cheekiness, his amazing choice of words (quite unusual for a fellow at his age) or his statement's content that perplexed the car driver most, was high above Nathaniel's ability of judgement. Still, he

121

was amused to watch the lad's face. To hear himself being described as "this strange man in that weird white nightshirt" barely bothered the guardian angel these days; he'd long become used to it.

"Who are you talking about?" The accident's causer looked around and shook his head when he didn't see anyone.

"This *man*! Didn't you see him?" The boy stared at the place Nathaniel had just been in a second ago. "Where *is* he? He was standing there, right now..."

"I guess it's the shock. Come on, we're holding up the traffic."

Reluctantly, the small figure let himself be dragged away by the guy's strong grip.

"I *swear*! I *saw* him! He had this cool golden circle above his head, how'd you call it?"

"Do you mean a halo?"

"Yeah, a halo! He had such a thing – a *halo*, and he wore a white shirt like my grandma when she goes to bed, except it had no flowers and that stuff on it, but..."

"Of course. Calm down now. No more ghost-stories." The man had apparently grown impatient.

"No, he wasn't a *ghost*. He was an *angel*!" the boy insisted.

"And I am Santa Claus..." The fat man rolled his eyes.

"Judging from your *proportions* you're not so far away from the truth" the boy giggled. The other swiftly turned around and fiercely faced the child.

"*What* did you just say?" he yelled.

Embarrassed, the little one held his hand in front of his mouth. "I don't know! I didn't *want* to say it! It wasn't *me* who said that! I can't explain what..." he stuttered.

"Being as smart-arsed as you are, you can't probably be harmed in any way. So, let's forget all about this, will you? I go my way, you go your way, and we'll hopefully never meet again."

The adult heaved his heavy body behind the stirring wheel and banged the door shut behind him. Then he drove off.

Nathaniel silently reappeared beside the boy. "Since there's no hell but only heaven, you won't be lucky enough to *never* encounter this... this *man*" – Nathaniel pronounced the last word with an unhidden revulsion in his voice – "again. But chances are not bad that you won't meet him in *this* world." He chuckled.

"Where did you go when I told him about you?" the boy, whose name would later turn out to be David, wanted to know.

"Nowhere. I just made myself double-invisible."

"Double-invisible? What does that mean?"

"During this whole wicked situation, I was invisible to everybody except you. So, I was *once*-invisible to every eyewitness. And when you started talking about my being there, I resorted to another little... let's call it *trick*... and made myself invisible even to *you*. You've got maths at school, I figure? They'll probably have taught you by now that two times one makes two. So, two times *once*-invisible makes *double*-invisible."

"Okay, but..."

"No more questions, please. This business is quite intricate. Besides, there are some rather strict rules I've got to obey, which don't make it any easier, you see?" The angel took a deep breath.

"Just one more thing – was it you who made me say that about his portotions?"

"*Proportions*, you mean? You caught me, that was indeed my doing." Nathaniel cackled.

"Cool!" David marvelled. "And what's your name?"

123

He looked the heavenly being straight into his sky-blue eyes. His interest wasn't playacted, the angel sensed.

"Nathaniel."

"Thank you, Nathaniel. Thank you for saving my life." He stretched out his tiny, soft hand to touch the grown-up, but the latter had already vanished.

Sitting behind his desk once again, Nathaniel sighed heavily. Why did such experiences always make him so sentimental? "I'm not a *softy*, for Christ's sake!"

"PARDON ME?!" The loud, vibrating voice took the guardian angel by surprise.

"Eh? I didn't use *Your* name, my Lord, did I? What's the big deal *now*? Has there been *another* enactment in the time of my absence?!" Certainly, the other one would realise his sarcastic intonation.

"EXACTLY. RULE NUMBER 289 406."

"Oh *no*..." Nathaniel banged his head on the wooden table.

"NATHANIEL, I KNOW YOU'RE UPSET. BUT REMEMBER – YOU DO USEFUL THINGS. YOU HELP KEEP THE WORLD IN BALANCE. YOU ARE NEEDED. EVEN IF ALL THIS MIGHT SEEM MEAN-INGLESS OR EVEN ABSURD TO YOU, IT ALL HAS ITS REASON. THE RULE'S PURPOSE IS NOT TO IRRITATE YOU, I ASSURE YOU."

After a short pause, in which neither Nathaniel nor the other said anything, the faceless voice continued: "HERE I HAVE SOMETHING YOU MIGHT ENJOY. IT'S A PRAYER I JUST RECEIVED."

Out of nowhere, a rolled-up parchment dropped on the desk. Carefully, the angel opened it and read it, frowning.

"WHY DON'T YOU READ IT ALOUD?"

"Why should I?"

Instead of a clear answer, he received an advice: "DO NOT UNDERESTIMATE THE POWER OF SPOKEN WORDS. SO, I DEFERNTIALLY ASK YOU TO FOLLOW MY REQUEST."

"If I have to…" Nathaniel cleared his throat.

"Dear God,

I am the boy who wasn't run over by a car today. Everybody calls me Dave – that's short for DAVID – but I think You know that, because in church they always say that You know everything. I met this man in my granny's clothes whose name is Nathaniel. At least he said Nathaniel was his name, but I'm not sure about that, because he was a bit peculiar. He was really nice, though. I wanted to ask him if my guess at his being an angel was right; unfortunately I forgot. If he is an angel, then perhaps he knows You. Could You please tell him that it was really nice of him to save my life? It was so cool how he threw himself in front of that car! He'd make a great stuntman! You could also tell him that. My dad thinks it's always good to have a card up your sleeve – so if You give Nathaniel the sack he would have an idea about what job to take on. So, please give him my thanks. He's a good angel, maybe You could give him a candy bar. (If I have done something really good, my mother sometimes gives me a Mars bar, and I like that.) Yeah, that's why I prayed to You. I'll quit talking to You now, if that's okay for You.

Ah, I almost forgot – I'm sorry to have beheaded my sister Abby's Barbie doll, the ballerina-one. I swear it was an accident! And, by the way, I feel really remoteful (is that the word?)…"

At this point, Nat couldn't help himself and gave a

heartily laugh. Once he had pulled himself together, he read on.

"...I feel really remoteful for having exchanged the toothpaste for shoe polish. I admit that this was no accident, but I didn't want to make Mum angry, I thought that Abby would brush her teeth with it. But I guess I should have known that she wouldn't do such a thing. Abby hates brushing her teeth! Next time I will pay more attention and will see that nobody uses it but my sister, I promise! Okay, I have to make an end now. There's Power Rangers on TV and I don't want to miss it, because if I do, the other boys at class will make fun of me. And I don't like that so much. I'm sure You understand!

Amen."

Nathaniel looked up. He didn't know what to say.

"I WILL NOW LET YOU GO ON WITH THE EVALUATION. I JUST THOUGHT YOU NEEDED SOMETHING TO LIFT YOUR SPIRITS."

The angel smiled and shook his head. "He really knows how to wrap His employees around His little finger..." he muttered to himself. "Where was I? Ah, here. Anything I especially like about my job? Yes. Honest gratefulness as a reward. Right... *Is there anything you especially dislike about your job?"*

Without having to think twice about it, he scribbled: "I especially dislike the pain that's inextricably bound to my position, for I often have to stop heavy moving objects or to expose myself to extreme temperatures, such as heat and cold." Reconsidering the last five words, he thought better and crossed them out. "Extreme temperatures need no further explanation, I'd reckon."

Do you have any suggestions to improve your

126

own/general working conditions?

"I strongly recommend forbidding the usage of modern technology (i.e. MP3-Players, iPods, portable game pads etc.) in road traffic, since it disturbs minors' attention. Furthermore, I would really appreciate the introduction of cushioned, bullet-, water- and fireproof shirts."

Thank you for having dedicated your valuable time to completing this Evaluation. Have a nice day!

"How awfully *kind* of them!" Nathaniel snarled.

"*BEEP, BEEP, BEEP,*" his beeper went.

"What is it?" the guardian angel asked.

"Emergency!" a female shrieked.

"Case? Not *another* car accident?!"

"No."

"Thank God..." Nathaniel sighed with relief.

"MY PLEASURE!" the vibrating voice interrupted joyfully.

"This time it's no car you have to stop." The female seemed to think about the best way to deliver the bad part of the news. "I fear it's a... *lorry.*" Knowing that Nathaniel wasn't too fond of Christmas related commerce, she didn't add that it was loaded with chocolate Santas.

"What the hell did I *do*?" Nathaniel cried.

"NO SWEARING, PLEASE!"

"What have I done to deserve this?!"

Bang, bang, bang. Ouch. This desk was *really* hard. He'd better kick his harmful habit...

Dedication
TK– who never stops believing in me.
Reinaldo - who was an angel on earth, and the best piano teacher who ever lived.

Raphaela Bruckdorfer is a 21-year-old Viennese (Austrian). She is interested in almost every activity requiring creativity, especially writing. She has been writing (and "illustrating") her own stories for as long as she can remember. She loves reading, watching great movies, as well as listening to music and playing the piano.

She is currently studying "International Development" and "Psychology" at the University of Vienna. After that she wants to spend some time abroad, meet lots of people and get to know the world.

Love, Light and Evelyn's Angel

Norma Murray

Evelyn felt the chill creep up through her thighs until it reached her back and shoulders, a cold so razor-sharp that each of her movements came only with great effort. Standing at the scullery sink the cold seeped upwards through the stone floor, even the wooden board she stood on did little to halt its penetrating path. With her teeth on edge every time the enamel bowl grated on the surface of the sink, she stretched and cursed; she'd let the fire burn low in the grate and now, with only enough wood to coax it along, there was no warm water left in the tank. If he wasn't too tired, if this time he came straight home, maybe he'd fetch in some more logs.

She tried rinsing what she could off the children's plates by running them under the cold tap, but the water chilled her wrists so they stiffened and ached. In any case it would soon be too dark to fetch any wood. Leaving the scullery door ajar she checked on her two small daughters. Made quiet by the increasing shadows in the darkening room, they sat silent, close together on the rug, feet straining towards the fire, absorbed in watching the dying embers.

Swallowing back a sigh, she shook the lamp, relieved the slight sloshing meant at least they'd have enough oil for some light that evening. Next, disregarding the pale glow that came from beyond the window, she took a spill of wood from the box on the mantelpiece, and caught a flame from the fire, cradling it with her hand. The lamp flared up briefly, filling the room with a sour yellow hue, before she turned the wick down low. Only now she peered out through the glass, then with a half smile, pulled the curtains not quite closed. He'd be home soon, if she left a gap – maybe this time he'd see the shimmer and understand.

Coaxing another spill, she carried the flame back into the scullery and, taking care not to burn her fingers, lit the single gas ring. With every sound in the room magnified by the quiet, she enjoyed the hissing and popping from the gas and its cool blue glow suited her thoughts. She picked up the kettle waiting on the draining board and by instinct filled it from the tap. With the light from the circle of gas and a glimmer coming in from the room next door, the scullery seemed almost cheerful, though the chill still seeped up from the ground making her legs ache.

A faint click as the kettle expanded told her it was warming. On the first sparse hiss of steam, she shook a handful of soda onto the plates, then poured out the nearly boiling water into the bowl, before refilling it again. He'd want tea when he came in. But she didn't put it back on the gas. Not yet. Steam from the washing up bowl gave off a faint metallic smell. Slipping her hands into the transient warmth of the water, she felt its brief luxury and closed her eyes, absorbed for a moment, before washing the plates. The knives and forks jangled against the sides of the bowl as she scooped them together and dumped them in a pile on the draining board.

Now came the point she was waiting for. With sleeves pushed well above her elbows, she bent her arms and plunged them into the warmth. As the glow spread, peace welled throughout her body; her thoughts stilled at last and she closed her eyes and rested her head against the white tiled wall by the sink. Her mind drained of everything, children, the cold, her husband and the angel that had appeared to her again that morning. She didn't hear her husband's steps up to the back door, so the click of the latch made her jump. As the door flew open, the mood changed.

"What the hell are you up to woman, wasting gas in the dark?"

At the sound of their father's voice the girls rushed to him, noisy, animated, clamoring to be picked up. He dropped his coat and cloth bag on the floor and, bending down, buried his face into their warmth. Then, after turning up the lamp and flooding the table in a pool of unforgiving light, he faced his wife.

"Well, where's my cup of tea then, eh?"

Saying nothing, she unrolled her sleeves down over her reddened arms and buttoned each cuff with care. Bending down to pick up his coat, she held it closely to her chest. It smelt of sawdust, earth and snow, the world outside.

Turning her face towards the window, she whispered, hardly daring to form the words, "I saw it again today. It's waiting for you out there. If only you'd look, maybe you would see it too."

"I said, where's my tea? You've almost let this fire go out again."

Hardly daring to smile, she glanced once more in the direction of the curtains. Emboldened by the light beyond the gap, she put out her hand towards the lamp.

"I'll turn this down. It's out there, see, still glowing in the tree."

"Dammit woman! Leave the lamp alone." He leant forward as if to seize her hand, thought better of it and spun round. Picking up the poker he attacked the last remaining embers in the grate and beat them small, to glowing coals. The children, abandoning their places on the rug, drew back as one. They hid in silence well beyond the radiance of the lamp.

Exasperation making his voice sound harsh and cruel, he shouted. "I tell you woman, there's nothing there. No lights, no angel voices. This has to finish Evelyn. Stop

131

right now! Already they're saying in the village you're sick. You're seeing things. You're going round the bend."

The space chilled between them. The warmth in the room drained away, as surely as if the back door had blown open. She sank into a chair and wrung her hands, overwhelmed by the weight of his displeasure.

It is there, she persisted to herself. I know you said it's only snow and snow refreshes the ordinary, but there really is an angel. If only you'd look out of the window you'd see its wings, outlined in the birch tree. He looked at her strangely and she wondered if she was saying the words aloud.

"That's enough of that," he snapped, this time more uneasy than unkind, and throwing down the poker in the hearth, strode past her. Wrenching the curtains wide apart he stared into the night and cried. "Just take a look." The light from within the room blocked out the scene outside. He turned round to face her, his reflected image mirrored in the glass. "See, there's nothing there my love. No angel, nothing but trees, and wood and snow." She jumped up from the chair and caught his arm. Pulling his hand towards her, she held the hardened palm against her cheek.

"Turn out the light my darling, then you'll see."

"I'm tired, I'm cold. I want some tea" he said again, pulling away. "The kettles not even on the ring. I need some food. You make a meal for me; I'll fetch us some wood."

They ate in silence, not even the raging fire in the grate could melt the frost that formed around their hearth that night. Hardly daring to whisper their "goodnight" the children scurried off to bed. Their father watched them go, then pulling on his coat went out the door soon after. She dimmed the lamp and waited until all grew dark and silent. Fuelled by a waxing moon, the light in the birch tree grew stronger. *Melt the wall of ice from his eyes. Open his mind and let him see*, she pleaded. Straining all her wits, she listened for a reply, but the angel only watched, unsmiling. Falling snow in the garden muffled all sounds.

Her husband came home late and beery. Already she lay in bed, fearful of his chill embrace. They slept, their bodies close, not touching. Sometime before first light she felt him stir, and then slip noiselessly out from his side of the bed. She heard the gentle pad of strong bare feet across the bedroom floor. She sensed him look out of the bedroom window, pause, then walk slowly down the stairs. Turning swiftly, she nuzzled deep into his heated, vacant space. She hugged herself, all but awake and conscious of his lingering warmth. He must have seen the angel, just beyond the bedroom window. How could he now deny its light? If only he'd listen to her, try to understand, all could be restored between them.

Cocooned and caressed by his body warmth she let the undertone of voices roam around her head, and there she lay, mid-way between wake and sleep. The click of the back door latch made her start. She felt unease. When the door banged shut, alarm had her clambering from the sheets.

The cold of the lino shocked her feet, but all was as before; the angel was still there. Its wings, motionless and silent, strung up so beautiful among the branches. Its face, formed from the purest of snow, a mask of shining white. She felt its peace, relaxed, sat on the bed, pulled on her slippers, satisfied; her husband was only getting wood from the shed, to make the house warm while they ate their breakfast.

She heard the children stirring in their room. She must get them dressed, put on some clothes herself. Half out the bedroom door she stopped and thought, just one more look, one tiny peep.

"No! No! No!" His feet were indelibly printed on the snowy path. Her man stood, axe in hand at the base of the tree. At the first blow biting deep, she caught her breath but made no sound. At the second, the angel shivered, shattering as it fell. The snow slipped with it from the branches until it lay spoiled and trampled on the ground.

When he came in for his breakfast he was smiling again. The armful of logs he threw hissed wetly down before the hearth. His laughing face aglow with triumph, he reached out and coiled a strong arm around her waist. "What's this, not dressed yet?" He pulled her to him, kissing her fondly on her forehead. He crowed, "No more of your nonsense, eh? I've cut that old tree down. It was making the cottage too dark. It's a bit wet but it'll burn." Half apologetically he laughed, "That's all we need isn't it Evelyn love, a bit of warmth and light?"

He leant forward, intent to kiss her mouth. Recoiling from his lips, she pushed his face from hers, fluttered her hands against her chest, breathed hard. "Yes," she said, but her eyes no longer saw his face. "For the moment we have warmth." The voices in her head came louder: *But what will you do Evelyn, now that all true love and light has gone?*

She sat down in a chair and stared out towards the day, so much darker now the tree was gone. He made some tea and fed the girls. He moved her nearer to the fire, now burning fiercely in the grate. He wrapped the children in their coats, and said, "Go kiss your mother," she turned and kissed her girls and raised her hand in parting as he led them out the door.

"Get dressed my love," he called. "I won't be long away."

She mouthed the words "Goodbye." And felt an icy blast, then they were gone.

The cold crept upwards through the floor. She turned her chilly face towards the glass. Come back, don't leave me, she implored. Please don't go. But only broken brushwood lay amongst fallen snow, muddied and soiled by booted feet.

She wasn't aware how long she sat undressed. The fire burnt out but still she didn't mind the cold. A knock on the front door made her jump. It came, polite at first, then hammering loudly and voices shouting. "Let us in Evelyn." An icy blast again. A woman, dark and stern stood, not quite smiling, with her companion, burly, tall and strict. "We are your friends. We've come to help you, dear," they said. Their boots made muddy puddles on the floor. "Now get your coat. You have to come with us."

Evelyn looked up, amazed, "But I'm not dressed." She spread her hands downward, held out her nightgown showing what she meant. "No matter, dear. The car's outside." The black crow woman held Evelyn by the arm. Taking the coat left hanging on the door, she threw it round her shoulders.

"She's only got her slippers on. The snow?" the tall man said.

"She's too far gone. I doubt she'll feel it, but get them if you must."

They found her shoes and he said, "Now hurry up and put these on. Haven't got all day you know." Evelyn felt anxious but obeyed.

Her husband joined them by the door. His face as white as snow; his eyes were red. "It's for the best." he said. "You'll soon be back." Exchanging swift glances the custodians led her past. When she touched her husband's arm, he trembled at her stroke and turned his face aside.

"They'll make you well my darling," he called out.

The car door slammed shut and she was gone.

"She's let the fire go out again," he cursed. "It's tea time and she wasn't even dressed." He stirred up the embers, coaxed them with some twigs. He fanned a flame; it burned not gold, but blue. The room shone with a silvery glow. He thought about his wife, his children, gone to stay with friends. He'd miss them both, but still, it's for the best. She wasn't well. She'd started seeing things, heard voices coming from her head. He went into the scullery, lit the gas, put on the kettle ready to make tea. "It's time I had my meal; I wonder what she'd cook? But still I'll make myself some toast and boil an egg, but first must draw the blinds. Light the lamp, to cheer the place up a bit."

He poked the fire again and briefly enjoyed its warmth then, drawn towards the window he looked out. The night seemed bright. It must be the moon, he thought, no star can burn like that. He shivered. "More snow before the morning, that's for sure," he spoke out loud. His lonely voice bringing no comfort or relief. A birch tree, the closest to the gate was moving even though there was no wind. He watched the angel land like snowflakes in the tree. He heard a voice say softly in his head. *She wasn't mad you know, not crazy, barmy, like they said, but precious, given different sight.*

He left the curtains open all that night, the fire burned low, the lamp unlit. He sat upon her chair and watched the angel suspended in the tree, and wept.

Dedication
Dedicated to the memory of Penny Brohn (1943 – 1999) a woman of vision and courage. A pioneer in the holistic approach to the treatment of cancer, who set up the Bristol Cancer Help Centre, now known as Penny Brohn Cancer Care

When Norma Murray isn't struggling to keep the weeds at bay on her allotment, you'll find her making highly individual jewelry using her own hand made glass beads. But her real passion in life has got to be her writing. She is the author of a collection of short stories and is about to finish her second romantic novel. A keen participant in a Brighton based writing group, she is also a member of the Romantic Novelists' Association. You can read all about the trials of writing romantic fiction via her blog.

http://myhalfofthesky-lampworkbeader.blogspot.com

Fallen

Debz Hobbs-Wyatt

*The miracle is not to fly in the air, or to walk on the water,
but to walk on the earth.*

Chinese proverb

Everything falls.

Kirsty stands on the edge and closes her eyes. A bus
turns a corner onto a New York Avenue. A girl steps out
of a revolving door. Time counts down in last moments.

The girl wears a suit, light grey, brand new. And shiny
shoes. She has her head down as she steps out of the
building, clutching a pile of manila envelopes. As she
walks a single sheet of white paper flutters to the ground.
So now the girl bends, red hair swept into her eyes by the
suddenness of a fall breeze. The paper falls three feet from
where Kirsty stands.

Sunlight dapples the sidewalk, skipping a path across
the puddles. Traffic horns fill the morning air and brown
leaves scuttle like cockroaches along the sidewalk.

The whole time Kirsty watches. Kirsty always watches.

Now the girl reaches out her hand for the paper.

Kirsty counts.

One.

A shiny shoe steps off the sidewalk.

Two.

Stumbling. Sun bleaches everything. Blinded.

Three.

Fallen.

The girl doesn't see the bus but Kirsty sees. She sees
the air streaked red. The girl doesn't see the driver's face
but Kirsty sees. She sees his lips fall open in horror. The

138

girl doesn't see. Except for one thing: she might see the outline of a woman, in her twenties, standing on the edge of the sidewalk but only for a moment, a fractured piece of a final moment. And as she goes the girl thinks about her dog. They often think about their dogs.

She will be pronounced dead at 11.05 am but she is dead long before an official time is recorded. The young doctor who records it says he doesn't believe in anything, certainly not angels. He doesn't believe in anything he can't see. But he has seen Kirsty; he just doesn't know what she is.

Lemon drizzle sun, spearmint sky, now it's spring time. An old man shuffles along a path in Central Park and stops at a wooden bench. But he doesn't sit down. Not today. Today he holds still, as still as the late afternoon. Perhaps he listens to the finches in the trees, perhaps he knows. Or perhaps it's nothing at all.

Now the old man turns his head and for a moment his gaze seems to find Kirsty. Or maybe it isn't her he sees. Something registers in his face, his lips part, his eyes widen. Then it's over. It's over so fast the old man is dead before he hits the grass.

In his final moment he thinks of a woman, a woman Kirsty sees, but only with the transiency of a reflection, an image that's gone as quickly as the old man falling. It's a moment so brief she can't hold onto it.

And she feels joy, overwhelming joy. And when it's gone she'll ache for it. She always aches for it. Just as she aches to touch, to feel something tangible between her fingers. But even as she presses her hands to the cotton of the old man's shirt she feels only where he was.

Kirsty will wait for someone to find the old man laying face down in the park. And then she will wait for

139

another doctor, in another ER, to write down another time. Only then will she leave.

Kirsty doesn't remember who she was. She doesn't know what she is – only what she will become. The city is full of angels. But there is always room for one more.

Kirsty never sleeps and always sleeps. Kirsty knows everything and nothing. She knows her name and she knows this city. She knows buildings and faces and she knows sadness and joy but she knows all of this through snatches of stolen memories, fragments of something lost: mostly from the ones she watches.

The moon washes roof tops in milky silver. At the river voices carry on a summer breeze. The city buzzes; Kirsty holds onto it, embraces it. People cry out, some in anger, some in pain, some in joy – they used to sound the same. A woman sits in an empty park, but not the same park where the old man died.

"I know someone's there," she says. "You think I don't, well I do."

Kirsty inches closer, watches as the woman sits down on the grass, a brown bag rustling at her fingertips as she loosens a lid on a liquor bottle, takes a sip. Then she looks in Kirsty's direction. "Oh they be saying I'm crazy," she says, "but I ain't, ya hear me. I been feeling you lot since I was knee-high to… well whatever it is you're knee high to."

Kirsty knows she has watched her before, heard her say this before but she doesn't know when. It's as if everything has become a déjà vu. So she sits with her and watches as she takes another slug of something brown, sour, sticky. She knows her heat rests between them like a blanket, but she can't feel it, only the memory of it. Kirsty follows the woman's gaze towards the river, the skyline

140

with its jagged edges. She senses a longing for something she can't place. So they sit in the silence of another day wearing out, watching the skyline bruise purple and pink and yellow. And they listen for the city's pulse. It is never truly silent. The only silence Kirsty knows is the silence of a final moment. Before the singing.

"You're a rookie," the woman suddenly says.

Kirsty turns to look at her face, but never in their eyes. She has done it before, trying to find their joy but finding only pain. So now she looks at her face. She studies the broad shape of her African-American nose, much like her own, and the fullness of her lips. But she doesn't look into her eyes.

"I know you ain't the one that's come for me," she says. "No Sir. They don't send trainees for that. I know that much. You gotta get your wings first." She laughs at her own words, a throaty laugh and then she coughs: deep hacking coughs and Kirsty reaches out to hold onto her but she pulls away.

Now Kirsty watches her lift the bottle and take another mouthful. She watches her screw the lid back on with trembling fingers and she watches her lift her face into the breeze. Kirsty does the same. She closes her eyes at the same time and remembers the feeling of heat, the feeling of blushing cheeks, the feeling of touch – a momma's hands. Now all she sees is air, rushing towards her, hot, then cold. Then all she knows is silence. But she remembers the thud of a heart beat. Now the only pulse she feels is the city. It's how she still feels connected.

"No Sir, they don't send rookies," the woman says. Then she rests her bottle on the ground and spreads a black plastic trash bag on the grass, places another where the pillow is supposed to be. It's filled with newspapers.

Kirsty doesn't speak. She has no way to speak, except

only in thought. So she studies the woman's tight grey curls, her thrift store clothes, the way she cradles the bottle in its brown paper to her breast and rocks it gently.

"I don't know what happens next," Kirsty says, pushing the thoughts into the air. She thinks the woman looks at her but she says nothing. She has tried this so many times, especially at the beginning, except there is no way of knowing when that was, how long ago it was. She wanted so bad to make someone hear. But no one does. No one ever does, except at that moment, but it's so fast she can't be sure.

"I want to understand," Kirsty says.

The woman pats down her plastic blanket but doesn't speak.

"I want to know how you know I'm here."

Still she says nothing.

"I want someone to hear me."

Now the woman takes a final swig, opens her eyes real wide and smacks her lips hard, pushing out air.

"I have to go soon," Kirsty says.

But she doesn't go, not yet.

Kirsty stands beside the woman. She doesn't know how long, she has no concept of time. She stays until she sees her lay down, folding into herself, nursing the empty liquor bottle. Kirsty stays while she sleeps. She stays while the city sleeps. She stays until it's time. And it's as she leaves she hears the old woman say, "They can all hear you, Honey. But you got to figure things out first."

The moment dissolves leaving behind a millions questions – but there is only one answer.

Now Kirsty is above the city for the sunrise. It's when Kirsty sees them clearest of all. She sees and she feels and for a moment she knows everything. And it's when she knows where to go and what will happen, whose name

will be signed next to a time on a sheet of paper in an ER.
But it wasn't like that for Kirsty.

An old woman wakes up in a park. A boy plays on a swing.
A parent looks at a photograph. It's raining. Soft summer
drizzle that washes colour into the anodyne city. The
woman stands very still at the window, the photograph
clamped between her fingers, but her eyes look out over a
backyard where the little boy plays. He holds onto the sides
of the old swing, kicks with both feet and then he puts his
head back, catching rain with his tongue. As the woman
stands at the window perhaps she thinks he will fall but she
doesn't go to him. She doesn't move. All she does is watch.
    And Kirsty watches too. Kirsty always watches.
    Kirsty stands by the swing with its rusty metal frame.
She has been here before but she doesn't know when. She
sees the shadow of the woman at the window. She hears
the creak of the swing. She sends out her thoughts, slows
the swing, wraps the child in a protective bubble and
wonders if she can keep him safe. And the whole time the
woman stands at the window. Now Kirsty closes her eyes
and aches for the feel of rain, the rush of air, a momma's
embrace but all she feels in this moment is overwhelming
sadness. She wants to leave.
    But she can't leave.
    So now Kirsty stands with the woman at the window,
shoulder pressed to shoulder and they watch the little boy.
Perhaps the woman feels someone at her side, perhaps she
only wishes she did. The little boy still has his head back
and he swings his feet, but the swing goes slower now. It's
a moment, a fleeting fragment of a moment but it's long
enough for Kirsty to know. She knows she has stood here
before. And then it's gone. Gone the way the sun bleaches
out faces.

But it's as Kirsty leaves she hears it. She hears the woman whisper a name. The woman stands at the window gripping onto the photograph, watching the little boy and she says, "Kirsty." And just as Kirsty disappears she adds, "Where are you, Honey?"

Kirsty often goes back to the river, sits with the homeless woman in the park, or sometimes in an alley or at the subway. She finds herself there, but has no way of knowing how or why. She is drawn to places, perhaps by the energies, just as she is drawn to the house with the swing. Sometimes it's raining, sometimes it's winter. Sometimes the little boy is asleep in a bedroom with rockets on the walls and a purple dinosaur on the duvet. Sometimes he isn't a little boy anymore. But like all moments with the living they are ephemeral, fleeting, like glimpses through a window. But sometimes, in the sunrise, she knows all the answers.

"They have to believe," the homeless woman tells her "It's the only way they can see you."

Kirsty asks the woman how she knows, what she knows, but she never says. So Kirsty presses herself to her as she sleeps, holds her hands as she trembles and watches her breath curling between them like pipe smoke. It's how Kirsty feels safe. She doesn't know why. The woman dreams of her momma and her poppa. And she dreams of a baby, her baby. Kirsty knows the baby is gone, and her momma and poppa are gone. She thinks she sees them in the sunrise. It's as if the whole world is waiting.

Just as Kirsty waits.

And Kirsty asks the woman how she knows so much. She asks her over and over. All she says is, "I know because I was one of them."

"You were an angel?" Kirsty says. "But how did you

come back? What happened to you?"

"I fell," she says.

Rain. Sheets of rain that cut across the air, as if it's slicing the day in half. Ice cold rain, dagger like. Kirsty is at the house with the little boy and the swing. He is in his bedroom; he has a fever, fidgets in his sleep. And in the quietest moment he says something, something Kirsty will always remember. He says, "Momma." She holds his hand, pushes cool air along the line of his cheek. That's when he opens his eyes. She thinks he sees her. She thinks he knows her. She thinks she wants to look into his eyes but right there with the rain rattling glass and tapping with its pitter patter footsteps on the roof, right there in a bedroom she knows but can't place, right there everything stands still. Everything is silent. Everything is clear. And Kirsty knows. Kirsty knows this is *her* son.

He calls out, "Momma. Momma." A shadow moves behind her. A voice calls out, a broken voice: "Kirsty, are you here?" Kirsty's tired fingers cling to the moment with blanched knuckles: gripping tighter. And tighter. And tighter. "Momma?" Kirsty whispers and she tries to look back, to look into the woman's eyes, but then, just like that, just like she did once before in another time and another place, Kirsty lets go.

Falling.

Falling.

Fallen.

Like leaves falling on a sidewalk where a bus turns a corner. Like an old man falling in a park. Like ticker tape falling in a downtown parade at a New Year celebration in a year she doesn't recall. Three, two, one... it's gone, like a balloon that bursts into a thousand pieces. Memories always shatter that way. But as she goes Kirsty sees the

145

woman in the doorway of her son's bedroom, she's holding something in her hand. She bends over the little boy in the bed. "Momma's gone," she says. "But grand-momma's here. Grandmomma won't let anything happen to you Harry. I promise."

Then she places the white feather on his pillow.

His name is Harry. Her son's name is Harry. She says it, tries to hold onto the feel of it. Mustn't let go. Mustn't.

"I won't let anything happen to you," her momma said. And Kirsty knows she said the same thing to her once. "I won't let anything happen to you, Kirsty."

But something did happen.

Kirsty falls into silence and wakes in another sunrise. But even when the sun bleaches out the faces she still remem-bers she has a son, she has a son called Harry and she remembers her momma. So now she knows why she goes to that house. But we she still doesn't know what happened.

Half a face. It's all that's left.

Gloved fingers move systematically tracking the path a bullet made. Trained fingers tracing gunpowder dust on mottled flesh. And later a young doctor covers the face and tells himself if he can't see it, it's not there.

Kirsty watches. Kirsty always watches.

Kirsty watches the doctor as he records the time. She watches him snap off his gloves. And she watches him wonder why a seventeen year old boy would take a gun, hold it to his own head and make his brain explode into a million pieces. Kirsty knows he wonders what the boy's last thoughts were. And he wonders why today? Why not yesterday? Why not tomorrow? Why?

He tortures himself with questions. He always tortures himself with questions. But he never questions why there is a young woman in his ER. Sometimes she's perched at the end of the bed, sometimes in the doorway, sometimes a reflection in an X-ray. He pretends he doesn't know who she is. And like today he pretends he doesn't see.

Next to the time on the piece of paper the doctor writes 'suicide.'

"We all make choices," the homeless woman told her once, "we all have free will."

"Yes," Kirsty said.

Now she thinks she understands.

Kirsty doesn't leave the ER, not yet. She watches the young doctor. Four more people die in the room. It's what he calls a bad morning. But she knows he thinks about her: about the ghost in his ER. She sees the way his face twists from a memory he pushes away. She knows it has something to do with her. So she stands in the doorway and watches as he throws swabs into the clinical waste and looks at the table with its blood splatters, like a flick painting. There are voices in the hallway, someone moans in pain and at the far end of the corridor doors swing open and another gurney rattles over a shiny floor. But right now, in this moment the doctor is alone.

Except he is never alone.

He sits with his head in hands and Kirsty stands behind him. She knows it's time to leave but as she does she whispers and the doctor lifts his hand to his cheek. She says, "I need you to show me."

Kirsty's poppa was white. "White as a ghost," her momma used to say. "And handsome too. *Real* handsome." Kirsty knows this today. She knows it as she stands in the sunrise and even when the sun comes she still remembers. Later she stands at the house where her momma flicks through old photographs in an album she was once too afraid to open and Kirsty sees her poppa's face. *"Real* handsome," Kirsty whispers and she sees her momma turn her head. Then she sits and she watches and she looks towards the garden and the swing and she knows. Kirsty remembers that day. She remembers this house. She was a little girl. She was playing on the swing. She can feel the air against her cheeks. Kicking legs, leaning back the same way Harry does. Higher. Higher. A phone ringing in the house. Her momma standing at the window. Potatoes burning dry on a stove.

And later Kirsty ran back to the house where her momma was still standing at the window, cheeks pinched tight with dried tears. "You poppa's dead," she said. "Something exploded in his head," she said. "You're poppa's dead."

Kirsty remembers the way it played like a classroom mantra: "You're poppa's dead. You're poppa's dead. Something exploded in his head..."

Bang.

Kirsty has seen aneurisms. She knows what happens. And it's nothing like the boy in the ER. Her poppa loved them; he would never have chosen to leave.

"Not everyone gets to choose."

It's something the homeless woman told her.

Now Kirsty thinks she knows why she finds herself standing over the body of a seventeen year old boy with gunpowder on his fingers.

"We don't always make the right choices," she says.

There are many photographs in the room where her momma sleeps. Her poppa, Harry, her. But for a long time she knows her momma couldn't look at them. "Everyone leaves," she told Kirsty once, a long time ago.

"Where do they go?" Kirsty said.

"They become nothing," she said. "Nothing." Then she'd looked right into the face of Poppa on the wall and said, "And all they leave behind are photographs to show they were here."

"What about me?" Kirsty said.

Her momma looked right at her then and cupped her hands over hers, as if she was holding a baby bird and she said, "I guess they leave the best parts behind."

Kirsty can't find the homeless woman. She can't remember how long it is since she saw her. She wants to tell her she remembers who she was, her momma, her poppa, Harry. That sometimes in the sunrise she sees herself falling. Stretching out her arms like wings and letting go. And she sees her poppa with his arms out, waiting to catch her. But instead she is drawn to endings: joggers in parks clutching their chests, old people in hospital beds, pile-ups on freeways, children with cancers and teenagers at parties who never think of consequences. Old, young, not yet born – doesn't matter what you are.

Kirsty stands with them. She watches what the others do and does the same. She's learned to hold their hands and tells them: "Don't be afraid."

It's something her momma said to her after she had Harry. She thinks of it now as she stands in the quiet of an empty side street looking for the homeless woman. She often walks the city at night. She remembers a room, a baby crying in a crib and her momma saying, "People get depressed. It happens sometimes after you've had a baby. You'll feel better soon, Kirsty."

"But what if I don't?" she said.

Fall. Leaves scurry along edges and turn corners on busy sidewalks. Children carve out pumpkin heads and dream in candy. And Kirsty watches a little boy through a classroom window. She watches Harry as he talks to the teacher. She aches to touch him. She knows she wasn't herself that day; she would never have chosen to leave him. How could she *ever* choose to leave him?

Kirsty remembers in painful fragments. Fragments of time she puts together. She remembers most things now. But not everything.

Sometimes she visits the past. She has seen the day she told her momma she was having a baby. It was her seventeenth birthday. And she remembers the way her momma held onto her and said she didn't have to tell her who the poppa was. Not if she didn't want to. Not if it was one of them *no-good-time-wasting-good-for-nothing-will-never-hold-down-a-good-job-kinda-boys.*"

She never told her she was wrong about that. She never told her he didn't even know there was a baby. She never told her how she made him believe she didn't love him. How she watched him as the yellow taxi pulled away and she stood on the sidewalk, his face pressed to the window, his lips parted, mouthing the words, "Don't do this."

There are many types of lie, and this was the best kind. She told herself this. She told herself as she pushed silent screams into a pillow. She told herself she did it for him. She did it so she didn't have to spoil two lives. White lies are the good kind. It's something her poppa told her.

"White lies are like angels," he said. "They stop people getting hurt."

"Do you believe in angels?" she'd said.

The ER is quiet. Outside it's dark but soon birds will sing in trees and a whisper of white light will perch at the edge of a new day. Kirsty watches cleaners with mops and buffers that glide effortlessly across shiny floors. She hears keys jangle in pockets and smells coffee in the air. She watches people sleep restlessly, she goes to them, places her hands on them and calms their storms. She hears the rhythmic bleep of machines and watches white lights move across black screens. But if she stands still – real still – she sees the others. Waiting. Like her. It's the busy time. She bathes in the joy of final moments and she always asks the same thing: "What is your last thought?"

Sometimes they say their children's names or Momma or Poppa or Uncle or Auntie, Brother or Sister.

Sometimes they say their pet's names.

Sometimes they say the names of their husbands or their wives or their lovers.

But one thing she knows for certain: everything is about love.

"Love is what draws you to them," the homeless woman tells her. "And it's what keeps you here."

As she stands in the waiting room of the quiet hospital Kirsty remembers a school, standing on a line on a field watching Harry play soccer while the other mommas waved and yelled and said, "Good job." But she always stood still. She always watched the poppas, how they ran and hugged their children, telling them how proud they were.

She remembers a birthday party, eight candles, children on the swing and her standing at the window. It was as if she was watching from the outside. It's as if she's always watched from the outside. Maybe she was waiting for an angel to take the hurt away. She was supposed to feel better. It's what her momma always told her. "Take the pills, Kirsty. You'll feel better tomorrow Kirsty. Maybe a job in the city will help you Kirsty."

151

It was a good job; it was a chance for a better life. Meet new people.

She wanted her momma to be right.

Kirsty remembers the first day in her new job. She remembers how she stood with her head pressed to the glass, looking down at people as small as flies, office sounds buzzing around her, people laughing, phones ringing, the printer spewing out paper and all she could think about was what it felt like to fly.

Now Kirsty presses her face to another window and watches the young doctor tap at a computer keyboard. He is hunched over. He rubs his hands across his eyes. So Kirsty goes to him, stands behind him. He looks back at the patient record on the screen and that's when she knows he sees her; he sees her reflection but it's only for a second, less than a second and he'll try to tell himself it's all the crazy hours he works, that it messes with his head. Kirsty presses her hands to his shoulders. "Show me what happened," she whispers. "I need to remember." He lifts his head, in her direction. He sucks in a deep breath. He looks back at the computer. "Why did I do it?"

There was a note. She sees it now as she stands with him. A note with the word sorry written over and over, in smudged ink. She left it in a drawer.

It was the note her momma found.

She watches the doctor's fingers tap at the keys, fast, furious. Faster. Faster.

"Show me more," she says again and now she presses her lips to his cheek and she sees something change in his face. She holds time still, holds his head in her hands and waits for him to turn his head to hers. "I know," she whispers. "I know you believe."

And then, right then in the silence of the quiet hospital

152

she looks into the doctor's eyes, right into his eyes and she says, "I love you."

And it's in the doctor's eyes Kirsty finally sees.

Kirsty stood on the edge and closed her eyes. She tried to say goodbye, tried to push the words into a cell phone, a cell phone she held to her ear long after the connection was broken. But she did say, "Make sure Harry understands, Momma." She did say, "There's a letter in the drawer, Momma. And she did say, "Harry's poppa is a doctor now. The letter explains everything, Momma."

And just like that Kirsty undid her lie. She watched it unravel; she set it free like a feather floating back to earth.

Kirsty stood on the edge and closed her eyes. She pictured her momma's face that morning, standing in the kitchen, eyes glued to *Good Morning America*, they were saying something about elections and the mayor's two terms of office and the whole time acting like is was any regular morning. Kirsty kissed Harry's cheek; she imagines its softness now, brushing against hers. He wiped it away, rooted through his backpack and asked for cheese in his sandwiches. He didn't even look up when she left.

Kirsty stood on the edge and closed her eyes. She held out her arms, felt the air, the heat. She would jump. She would do it. She counted down her last moments.

One.

She thought of her momma and her poppa.

"Of course I believe in angels," her poppa told her. "Of course I believe."

Two. She thought of Harry. She will always think of Harry. Always.

Three.

She thought of the man she loved. As Kirsty stepped into the silence she thought of her young doctor and she said his name. She whispered it so softly but she hoped wherever he was he would hear.

The young doctor stands in a deserted room in a quiet ER and he cries. He cries for the young woman who touched his cheek and whispered, "I love you." He cries when he thinks of the older woman who came to his ER and handed him a letter, a letter he still has: it's folded in his wallet, an address he knew from the past, the name of his son. She named him after him. He remembers when the older woman told him they would probably never find Kirsty's body in the debris at Ground Zero. He cries for the son he's been too afraid to visit, but he will. He will now. He thinks what just happened in his ER is a sign.

Kirsty stands with him as he cries. For a moment she sees another place, by the river the same place where she has looked for the homeless woman. In this place Kirsty stands at a wall where people write messages to those that have passed: to firemen, to cops, to mommas and poppas and aunties and uncles and brothers and sisters, to husbands and wives and lovers. Behind the sea of dancing tea light flames she sees photographs. Among them there is one of her. And she knows her momma puts flowers there. And she knows Harry puts flowers there. And now she knows he will put flowers there, the other Harry.

Kirsty knows everything now.

Kirsty knows why there was no time written on a piece of paper in an ER. She knows that she didn't choose to leave them. But she did choose to fall. And as she fell she chose to become an angel.

Soft clouds roll along the edges of a new day. Kirsty sits in the park by the river. She doesn't know how long ago it was she stood in the Emergency Room and told the young doctor she loved him. Or how long ago it was she saw him at the house, crying on the shoulder of her momma: two shadows standing together at a window. And how later she saw him pushing her son on the swing.

Today Kirsty sits in a park. She has waited a long time, searched for her friend in all the city parks and in alleys and in the hollow rattle of downtown subways. But today she finds her. Today she sits with her on a plastic blanket. And she waits. As she waits she looks at the sky, at chalk trails left by airplanes, at the space where the towers used to be. She thinks about the day she fell from the sky. This time when she closes her eyes she sees the way the sunlight sparkles like a million fragments of glass. And she hears the singing. She hears it as the sun rises higher over the city and she is filled with overwhelming joy.

"So how's it work?" she whispers. "You can just fall back to earth?"

"Ain't you learned nothing," she hears the old woman say. "You got to figure it out for yourself. And now you got your wings, you can figure out just about anything."

Kirsty waits. She waits for the city to wake up. For doctors to prepare Emergency Rooms for whatever the day will bring. She waits for whatever comes next.

Across the city a grandmomma stands at a window and watches a little boy talking to his momma. He doesn't see her anymore. That's what he tells his grandmomma and his poppa. And his poppa always tells him: "You don't always have to see something to know it's there."

The young doctor hasn't seen Kirsty since the day she told him she loved him.

Kirsty lifts her head as the sunlight bleaches everything out. She holds onto the joy in the silence, she loses herself in the singing. Now she reaches for her friend's hand but feels only where it was. And she thinks, for a moment, a tiny splinter of a moment before the sunrise is over, she sees her standing in the light holding a baby, two shadows standing behind her. But then it's gone.

So now Kirsty waits. She waits for someone to find her friend in the park.

Only then will she leave.

Dedication

To angels that come with paws and pads and claws and beaks. Those here now: Cagney, Lacey and Rosie, and those passed, and especially for my parent's cat Cookie, who passed away this year but did make his 20th birthday

---

Debz Hobbs-Wyatt is a full time writer/publisher working from her home in the mountains of Snowdonia where she lives with her cats, Cagney and Lacey, and her cocker spaniel, Rosie. She has recently passed her MA in Creative Writing at Bangor University and has had several short stories published. She is also seeking an agent for her fourth novel. Debz is a partner and the publicist for Bridge House Publishing, Editor for CaféLit and the Director of her new venture Paws n Claws Publishing and the PAWS workshops scheme. She is also the editor for this collection!

www.debzhobbs-wyatt.co.uk
www.pawsnclawspublishing.co.uk

The Angel Stone

Holly Stacey

I looked around at all the black dresses and slick handbags and felt sick to my stomach. They all peered eagerly at one another, like carrion crows ready to pick the carcass of my grandmother clean. Only it wasn't her carcass they'd be picking at now; it was her estate. Her five point two billion pound estate. I shuddered. Two of my cousins looked over and nodded as it I was in the cool crowd. I glanced away. They'd not get any more information out of me and I had no desire to let them exhale tobacco smoke in my face.

My mind drifted back to last summer when all of us stayed together at Gran's large house. Mike and George kept their distance, preferring to drink the champagne they'd found in the guest house and smoke our late grandfather's Cuban cigars. I'd stayed close to Gran. She'd said it was nice to have another woman to talk to. I'd laughed at that; I'd never been called a woman before. Even turning seventeen hadn't made me feel any more than just "a girl"...

"You're no longer a young lady, Anna." Gran said, "And anyone who says such words to you is talking down to you. Tell them to address you as Miss Stone."

I laughed at that too. It was a good summer, despite my cousins constantly getting into trouble and trying to hawk things they'd found around the house. It was then that Gran told me the legend of the Angel Stone.

"This has been handed down from generation to generation," she said looking me right in the eye. I looked down and in her palm was a shining ice blue stone about the size of a walnut. It was roundish and had a symbol

157

carved in the flattened bit near the centre with what looked like quartz.

"It's beautiful," I breathed. My eyes couldn't pull away from it and I began to feel like I was being rude. Gran chuckled.

"It has the power of the angels, passed down to mortals to help where it can. It likes you," she said. "Normally it doesn't take to new people, but I'm pleased it's taken to you." She gave my hand a quick pat and dove straight into the tale. "Legend has it that the Angel Stone was given to one of our ancestors to fight demons. The first woman in our family put it in a stave. She could, apparently, summon lightning with it and smite down evildoers." Gran chuckled at that and I imagined some barbaric woman riding like Boudicca in a chariot with lightning behind her. "Then the next used it in healing waters. She placed it in a spring fed lake and all who bathed in it came out cured."

"Or at least cleaner than they had been," I joked. But Gran's face didn't seem to share my humour. I realised then that she was dead serious and believed the stories.

She took a deep breath, gazing lovingly at the stone. "It skips several generations," she said. "Not everyone it takes to can harness its power or use it. I certainly couldn't."

Despite feeling uncomfortable about what Gran was saying, I kept looking at the stone. I couldn't break my gaze and I began to imagine what it would be like if the stories were true. Every part of me wanted to touch it. The power of the angels put into a stone... "Can I hold it?"

She nodded. I could tell even with my eyes locked onto the stone because I heard her eyeglass chain rattle. I held out my hand and she put the Angel Stone inside of it. My palm closed around it and I let out a deep breath. It was as if someone had turned on music – only it didn't feel like the tinny sound that comes out of my headphones, but a proper

158

full orchestra and it seemed to be coming from inside me.

It took all my willpower to hand it back to her, but the music stayed. She looked at me then and I knew we had a special bond – something beyond words. Just after that, my cousins burst into the room demanding lunch and Gran was whisked away into the kitchen...

I shook my head and looked at the grave. Gran was gone and whatever magic she'd had was now gone too. Someone next to me forced a cough. I knew from the smoke it would be one of my cousins, but I couldn't face looking up – I didn't want to see their smirks.

"Reading will be soon," said George, the eldest of my cousins. I took a deep breath and kept my gaze focused on the hole in the earth.

"I reckon I'll get at least one mil – how 'bout you?"

The earth looked damp against the shiny coffin and I wondered how long it would be before the veneer would wear away and the cold damp would leak into Gran.

"Um, hello?" He sounded annoyed. I heard another shallow cough and refused to look up at my other cousin who I knew was staring at me.

"C'mon Mike," said George, let's just leave her."

I don't know why Gran put up with them. They were like leeches – emotional and needy vampires that now wanted her estate. They'd probably get it too. I supposed that some part of her felt it important to protect every blood tie she had. Perhaps she felt that one day one of their children or grandchildren could inherit the Angel Stone and the magical powers that supposedly went with it. But the thought of something good coming out of my cousins just seemed ludicrous. I wasn't as generous and as giving as Gran.

The day passed; the people thinned out and then eventually dispersed out until there were just one or two distant relatives remaining. The sky darkened quickly and I was asked politely to leave, but I couldn't go. Not yet.

"It's just we've got ta fill in the grave," said a man wearing a high visibility jacket.

I could see the small JCB digger flashing as the driver looked towards us anxiously. "I'll not get in the way," I said. He looked both confused and frustrated but finally waved his colleague to bring the JCB over and begin filling in the grave.

I stepped a few paces back, but kept my eye on Gran's coffin, watching as the earth was shoved over it. The giant claw looked like an elegant and hungry creature, pushing its head against the mound of dirt, then pulling up and scooping. I liked it better with the mechanical digger than a man with a shovel.

They finished. The two men in yellow vests looked anxiously towards me, but eventually left and I was able to walk to the fresh grave and kneel by the stone. I put my hand on it and took a deep breath. The stone was cold. Cold like the earth.

Cold like the Angel Stone.

My heart skyrocketed. I could hear her. In my head. "Gran?"

I waited for about five minutes, but there was nothing – just a chilly evening breeze and the glimmer of the evening star. It hit me suddenly – that I was in a grave-yard alone and close enough to night that I should be worried. Not about ghosts; I have no fear of their wanderings and cold hands on my face, but the area was rough and the graveyard was a hangout for drug dealers and street gangs.

I knew Gran's voice was in my head. And that if she was still alive she'd be angry at me for lingering in a potentially dangerous place.

Get to the estate, her voice said. *You must continue with your duty.*

I couldn't help but smile. Even though she was only projected from my memories of her, it was just so Gran. Stretching, I walked towards my lone car – an old black ford focus with a dent in the rear (bought it like that two years ago for £300). My feet were aching from standing too long and the damp grass had managed to spread wetness all the way up to my knees. I can do this, I thought. I didn't just miss Gran; I had been avoiding the rest of the family too.

As I pulled into the wide drive leading up to the estate, I could already sense the greed in the air. I passed four cars parked up on the side of the road that I recognized and although there was ample parking at the estate, I also knew that some of my family wanted to make a quick exit as soon as they were awarded with their chunk of the fortune. The only reason there could be for those cars to still be there was that everyone was still waiting for the reading of the will.

"Anna, what took you?"

My aunt kissed the side of my cheek gently, but her eyes were shrewdly looking me up and down. I repressed a shudder but forced a smile. "I was detained," I said as congenially as I could.

They were all there – gorged and still drinking flutes of champagne. My stomach nearly heaved. It was as if they were celebrating. I bit my lip hard and sat at the back, determined to not look at anyone lest they see my revulsion.

"To my darling relatives," read a lawyer in a fancy suit, "to each of you I leave a small lump sum of £200,000. Invest it wisely and it will see you through." There was an audible intake of breath from the cousins.

161

£200,000 was pocket change to them and I knew they'd be taking legal action to get more. The lawyer continued. "The remaining bulk of my estate and savings is to be given to my favourite charitable trust." This led to some shifting of chairs and uneasy pulling of collars. The estate in itself was worth more than five million. I laughed as I imagined what would happen if the estate fell into the hands of a donkey sanctuary. I quickly quieted my giggles when I felt the ice pour from my relatives. "And finally, I offer the post of estate manager to my granddaughter Anna Stone with the provision she live on site in the two bed annexe that is situated on the estate. Her salary of £17,000 per annum to be generated from the trust." Now it was my turn to suck in my breath. My head seemed to want to drift off into unknown places. Free lodging and a meagre salary – albeit just the right wage to keep my more than satisfied. What had Gran been planning?

The lawyer snapped his folder shut and looked up at the ashen-faced crowd. "Well, that's that then. I have a cheque for each of you and will post them out at the end of the week. Miss Stone, if you could follow me please."

I could feel my cousins' eyes burning into the back of my neck. They wanted me to turn around and share with them that I too felt hard done by. To them, I was given a lowly post that only a groundskeeper should take. But I felt that Gran had blessed me. The memories stored up in that small two bed annexe would comfort me in the lonely years to come.

There was a lot of grumbling and one of the aunts paled and grabbed the back of the seat in front of her to keep from falling over, but I ignored them all and followed the lawyer. I'd always known Gran would provide for the family; she had an acute sense of duty to blood relatives, but this was a dig too deep as far as the cousins were concerned. She pretty much just told them to go out and get jobs, while still giving them a nibble of the estate's cash. Classic Gran. But I was curious about this whole trust idea – the lawyer didn't mention which charity it was going to.

We passed out through the front door and walked around to the annexe near the old stables. Neither one of us spoke and when we arrived, he just opened the door and gestured politely for me to go in. I'd been in so often before that it felt like home. One time, long ago when Gran had lots of guests at the house, she and I stayed in the annexe together and watched old horror films. It brought back such strong memories, I had to bite my lip to keep from crying.

"I'll leave you to it," the lawyer said. He turned and left. I didn't have the energy to question him.

It must have taken me at least two hours to reach the bedroom – for some reason I was just reluctant to go in there alone, but it was getting late and I wanted to rest before moving all my things in. There was a small packet on the bed with a note in Gran's handwriting. My mouth went dry. She'd meant for me to come here first, and I botched it.

"Anna," it read, "I know this may come as a shock to you, but I'd been planning for the event of my death for years. I like to keep my things in order and I'm sure you'll understand that I wanted to make sure all were provided for before I set to the trust."

My eyes were tempted to scan the letter to end the mystery, but I forced myself to read on.

"The estate is now registered in the Stone Charitable Trust. It is up to you to make of it what you will. You are the next chosen Stone to inherit not only the Angel Stone, but the power that goes with it. Do not be frightened and don't worry about not knowing how to use it – it will show you when the time comes. I love you and now I am with our parted family. We'll be watching over you. With all my blessings, Gran."

I put the letter down, trying in vain to gain some composure or to simply stop shaking. Looking at the window, I took a slow, deep breath. Her words slowly came back to me… words I'd dismissed at the time but felt powerful now. "The stone will sing to one in each generation and only one." The dark evening gave me no knowledge or insight – only my own refection staring despondently back at me. Wiping away a fresh tear I wondered how I could live up to such high expectations. How could I, just Anna, deliver what was needed to wield the power of the stone? I couldn't banish demons, there was no well or spring to make healing waters from. But she trusted me to know. I put away my doubt and tried to bury it deep. I could not let Gran down. If she thought I could do it, then I had to.

I wiped my eyes with a tissue and reached for the packet. I knew what it was before it fell from the wrappings; it was humming loudly. My confidence grew. Images of what I could do with the estate flooded my brain, as if the stone had always had its divine plan for me. I wondered if perhaps the stone did not just hold the power of the angels, but was in itself the spirit of an angel, guiding, as angels are said to do. As it fell into my hands, the humming changed into chiming music that only I could hear in my head, for it had chosen me in a long line of Stone women to make my mark on the world.

Dedication
Dedicated to Elizabeth Gunn, my angel and Gran who always inspired and never criticised, despite all my hairbrained ideas

Holly Stacey was born in southern California and spent most of her life dreaming about adventure and looking for things to dig up. She has two degrees in archaeology and has excavated Romans, Chumash, Picts, Anglo-Saxons, Celts, Vikings and Victorians – a pastime that has given rise to folklore and history inspired writing. She is now an editor for Wyvern Publications and writes young adult and teen fiction. For more about Holly's writing, read her blog on http://inkydoom.blogspot.com.

Meringue

Alison Wells

There was an angel at the end of the bed, she insists.

"Did you see it, when you came in?" she asks me, her thumb pressing fiercely into the back of my grasped hand, almost parting the metatarsals. I look down at her small white mop of a head. How is it she grows tinier every day but is taking so long to disappear?

"Did you see it?" she asks me again, agitated.

That's the words the nurses have for it. "She was very agitated yesterday evening" they tell me. It's like a code. They had to give her something, they say, to get her settled. No wonder she is seeing angels, between the drugs and the bags of marshmallows they hand out. Nice and easy to eat, they say, what with the sores on her mouth and the decrepit dentures.

Sugar rush, I say. Wired. One of the day's high points. Like Sasha and Natalie after a birthday party. I used to have to make them run around the garden fifteen times when they came home or they'd tear the heads off their Barbie dolls or send the dog loolah by tying one of my bras to its tail, usually one of the lacy ones which the dog then destroyed or embarrassed me with by leaving it in the next door's garden. There's no mistaking my bras, it's double d or die with me. Wouldn't go near those girls, though. They're all grown up now but they're like knitting needles. Went through that whole bulimia thing with Sasha a couple of years back. She swears she's stopped now but... mmm those marshmallows do look tasty.

"Can you hear me?" Mama asks.

She's picked that up from people saying it to her. They

all think she's deaf but she's always been like that. She only bothered to listen if you were deemed free of transgression. Forget X-Factor. Try guilt factor. Search and destroy self-esteem. Don't get me wrong, I'm not hung up about it, haven't gone the counselling route either. I am the enlightened consumer of self-help books. 'Eleven steps to self-esteem', 'Turn on the light for the child within'. 'Don't get sad, beat your old folks round the head with a hockey stick'. Just kidding on the last one.

"I hear you," I say to my dear old Mama. "But I didn't see anything."

I don't usually pay much attention, I find it easier to block out the extraneous (sounds like a medical condition) mad goings on in the world today. I can't count how many times one of the girls has said to me, "Did you see those guys in the park? They were dealing," when all I saw was the sun resting gently on the grass and a cocker spaniel christening a row of silver birch. Or that one time a lady's purse was snatched, right next to me on the 25A to Chapelizod.

"Did you see anything?" the lady said. "Did you see where the guy got off?"

Not at all. I was wondering if I'd missed the final of Britain's Got Talent and whether I'd be able to stop myself from lurching backwards if I got up and pressed the button before my stop.

"You ought to stand up straight" Mama rants, twisting my hand until all the blood goes out of it. "You're like the Hunchback of Nutter Damn, looking at the floor all the time. I warned you," she says, "I told you you'd never hold onto a man that way."

When you visit the very old, as you know, the same conversations come round and round like rolling news on the BBC. "Whatever happened to Uncle Marcus, did he ever give up the drink?" "Did I ever tell you about the time I cut off all my hair and left it down the back of the settee?" And her absolute favourite: "No man leaves you at the altar without a good reason, you must have done something."

Well it wasn't actually at the altar. It was two weeks before. As it happens I was trying on my wedding dress, the dressmaker had managed to let it out another two inches and I was just making sure I could get it on. I was looking in the full length mirror and lifting up my head (for once, to minimize the resting chin syndrome) and I was thinking "Meringue" and it was a light, gooey, happy feeling because I like meringue and I could see myself floating in a sweet, sugary, angelic cloud down the aisle of St Judes, and landing precisely in pump encased plump feet beside darling Richard, my own, finally, all six foot two of him and that's high not wide.

Everything felt just so and the cherry blossom had just come out and the street sweeper had been down earlier and sucked up all the cigarette butts and ripped crisp packets into its metal belly. The light was still lemon young, resting shyly on the tops of things, the houses opposite, the roof of the abandoned Fiesta in front of number 24. Shy the way you're supposed to be when you're not babe material (unless you mean that film with the pig in it) and the man you've fallen head over comfortable-walking-shoes in love with passes your cubicle on his way to the water cooler. Shy the way you're not supposed to pop up from behind the divider and ask him if he wants to go bowling next Tuesday. And then on Tuesday ask him if he's seen the remake of that classic 1970s sci-fi everybody's talking about and so on and so on it went until we were both well past shy and motoring before it got a chance to put the clamp on us.

So this morning I'm talking about. Everything felt just so. Absolutely. I could hear Sasha tearing up the stairs as usual. She does it a hundred times a day religiously. Stairway to Slim Heaven. She's supposed to go back down again but she burst in, barely puffed.

"Hey you look great" she said, very convincing.

She is a sweetheart, like her mother was. Sweet eighteen, ready for the off. She'll be okay. At least I've done everything I could to stop her world from shattering completely. Thin ice.

She held out the mobile handset.

"It's Richard" she said. "Wants to have a word." And her voice was round with giggles and optimistic as if she was still four and nothing bad had happened to her mum, my lovely big sister.

Richard was very apologetic in a formal kind of way, as if he was ringing up to cancel a cheque or a provisional holiday booking. You think you'd remember such a momentous phone call in detail but when I try to get a handle on it all I can think of are vague words like Regret, Inconvenience, Unable.

When I put the phone down I just kept thinking meringue, meringue. But it was a different kind of meringue – a meringue puffed up and expanded, doing the job of polyfilla, filling the hole of a gaping Why?

Mama is getting impatient. "I don't want to spend the rest of my life waiting for you to stop chewing" she says.

I cannot believe that she's ninety. Forty five she was when she had me as an afterthought or before she fought my dad off with the reinforced knickers and the garlic capsules. Now I'm forty five, just like she was and just like Suzie was too when it happened, so it all adds up doesn't it, multiplies by a factor of two?

Two who? Just the two of us, Richard and me, cleaved apart by the forces of inertia. He wasn't really sure if he wanted to trade in BBC4 for the Living Channel or eau de reheated casserole for rose water and ylang ylang.

Or just the two of us, Mama and me, factors of each other, factoring each other into our otherwise non-eventful lives. Well non-eventful is better than us holding both ends of a disintegrating phone line while I have to tell her that Suzie has killed herself and yes, she's dead, really dead and I don't know anything else and I don't know why (unless what happened with David hit her harder than we realised). And I don't know how those two beautiful little girls are going to do without her and I don't know why it was her, not me, when she was so much better, in every way, than I am. And you knew that, didn't you Mama? Told me that a thousand disheartening times.

Or the two of us, Suzie and Rosie, I don't know what else to say. She was just my big sister, fabulous, an angel, just so composed and forgiving and generous and dead. Pale white, white with the glory washed out in the blue light of the morgue. Blue eyes, blue lips, blue veins. In school they said "remember veins is like the French word venir, to come." The veins returning blood back to the heart for air.

Mama is on her way to the morgue but she's taking her time getting there. Has she forgotten what she asked me? I have. But she doesn't give in.

"The angel said he'd give you another chance" she says.

Is she talking about Richard or the angel? A chance to

live my life over? Why would I want that? I had my man, even if it was for just a little while and it was me he wanted, the bulk of me, the dimples where dimples shouldn't be, the sweat and the tears and the tablespoon of chilli in the bolognaise sauce. I had my children, well sort of, borrowed from Suzie until they were old enough to do without both of us. And they are fine, I can feel it, so I haven't slipped up there.

My hand is starting to get cold; she's holding it so tight. I let go on pretence of smoothing the bedclothes. I ask her if she wants her pillows straightened up. She mutters into her chin while I am doing it, worries the blanket hem between fingers as brittle as twigs. I have passed forty I am thinking, I am over the hill and bottom-shuffling down the other side on a cushion of rolling, unruly flesh. And ever now and then I get a tweak or an ache only it never goes away, never quite heals and my frown lines are like the gouges between the slices of a takeaway pizza. I look at my Mama with her chicken neck and her rheumy eyes and I wonder how it's possible to be ninety, another lifetime again of falling apart. How is it that her powdery skin doesn't just crumple away like Wensleydale, her frail bones collapse all at once, and the eyes that have burned forever snuff out, trailing wisps of toxic smoke?

"You must have done something" she persists, "for him to up and leave you like that, no warning," she leans forward.

I don't know why the blunt needle of her memory has her stuck in this particular groove on this run of the mill Monday. Maybe she misses Richard; he used to pop in with me at the weekends. Perhaps it's all to do with the familiar, perhaps because she's had to skip her usual routine, she's jumped into the next track on the LP – (does she know they don't make them anymore?)

Maybe she's still annoyed at herself for letting our dad give her the slip.

"Just popping out for the Sunday paper, want anything?" he said. He never came back.

Had a heart attack in front of the chippers at the age of 56. Never apologised or anything.

"Are you with me?" she says. She is staring at the foot of the bed. "Leaving those two young girls, his own flesh and blood. He was a great man, a lovely father" she continues.

"Yes, I'm with you Mama." Blind man's buff. Who am I reaching out to? "Are you thinking about Dad?" I gamble.

I take her hand again but she pulls it away, makes it into a fist and slams it down on the covers. I think of making a fist too or rather of cramming fistfuls of marshmallows into my mouth. I can picture myself with pink and white squidgy cubes falling out of a gaping tunnel in the middle of my mountainous face.

"I don't believe all that about another woman" she continues, directing her thoughts to the bedstead. Her voice has a pitch in it that makes my insides feel like a noodle dish that is being gathered up and eaten with chopsticks. It's the sound of a car in the wrong gear at a driving test, an excruciating whine that means you've failed.

"You must have driven him away, Suzie. David never would have gone otherwise. You never could get anything right, not like Rosie and now you see what you've done to her, saddled her with two teenagers and scared off poor Richard. Such a lovely man, Richard was."

Mama sinks right back into the pillows and they billow up around her like marshmallows. Or meringue. She is tired now and her eyelids start to lower like the metal tambours on shopfronts when you still want to look into them because there is something inside that you might want to buy but you just want to check first if the item is what you think it is and if the price is what you are willing to pay.

And when her eyes are closed, I keep sitting there and I look at her now that I can and I wonder how it is that Mama, Suzie, me and the girls so carelessly lost all our men and are left here waiting and watching, all except Suzie that is, well maybe Suzie is waiting and watching too.

And is it possible that all along Suzie thought that I was the good one?

The next time I visit, Mama is lying there, just the same, as if I had only slipped out for a minute.

They take me aside. They say it won't be long now, until she passes over. That's another one of their code phrases. You need to be on the ball if they say she's gone to sleep. Don't assume anything, listen for further qualifiers. "We did everything we could" (gave her the anti-agitation medication to get her to go off?). "She's gone to a better place" (more ambiguous, but she would tell me that sleeping is better than putting up with the noises Mrs Devlin makes when they are changing her into her nightclothes.)

I put my head up to her face and she is still breathing. She seems peaceful. Now I have begun to speak in euphemisms too, as if my mouth is full of something soft and sweet and sticky. I wonder how she can still be alive at ninety, how she must have had the antidote to the poison she carried round in her all those years. And as I think those thoughts something surges in her and she rouses from the deepest of sleeps. Her face creases with horror as she realises where she is, that this is the life she is still living. I move over to her and stroke her brow and the side of her head close to the departing hairline. I stroke her back to sleep as if she is an infant, plump with innocence and pleasure.

As she retreats into sleep she searches for my hand but her fingers only skim over the end of ice-cold digits.

"I've just remembered, Rosie" she whispers into the encroaching dark. "Suzie said that if anything happened to her, you'd be there to look over them."

And I did Suzie, I did my best and now they don't need me anymore and neither does Richard. Now there's only you left Mama.

I take one more look at her, scraps and sticks. I won't ever leave her. If she needs me, the nurses will tell her that I merely stepped into the next room.

When I return there is angel at the foot of her bed.

"Can you see it?" she asks me, her breath running out.

"Are there any marshmallows left?" she wonders, rambling. "Help yourself, Rosie. Help yourself." I shake my head but she doesn't notice.

Her face becomes bright, her features smoothing out like pouring sand. She almost rises from her bed, leans on one robust elbow. "You must see her" she says, "she's lovely, all dressed in white. I think I can hear her wings swishing."

"I can see her now" I say.

"Don't go away" she whispers.

"I won't" I tell her.

I stand watching over her as the lemon light filters into

the room and rests on everything. I pivot and swish. "Meringue" I think. "Meringue, Meringue, Meringue."

Dedication
To my mother Bridie Wells who has made a lifetime of caring and consideration for others and whose support is always steadfast

Alison Wells lives in Co. Wicklow with her husband and four young children. She was shortlisted for the 2009 Hennessy XO New Irish Writing Awards, The Bridport and the Fish Prize. Her short stories have been published in magazines, online and print anthologies. She is putting together a short story collection Random Acts of Optimism and has completed a comic novel Housewife with a Half-Life. She blogs at Head above Water: <u>www.alisonwells.wordpress.com</u>.

The Rescue

Katie Lilly

A shrill scream pierced the woods, rousing Cherrie from a deep slumber.

She pushed back the nettles from her face and struggled to her feet. Brushing the loose dirt from her body, she instinctively set off in the direction of the noise. She tumbled over fallen branches and rotting leaves, as her legs struggled to keep up with her thoughts. Another scream permeated the damp air, but it was stifled by the roar of an engine. Its fierce growl reminded her of a lion protecting its prey and she quickened her pace, pushing her way through the tangle of foliage towards the growing patch of daylight.

Cherrie emerged into dazzling sunshine and quickly covered her face, jumping back into the shadows. She rubbed her eyes until her vision cleared. She was in a lay-by, an expanse of grey gravel segregated from the road by a row of straggly shrubs. The place was empty except for a pile of discarded rags at the side of the tarmac. *Had she imagined the scream?* Cherrie stared at the rags, somehow drawn to them and, as she approached, they began to take shape. She recognised a protruding leg, an arm and a fuzz of blond hair. The bundle moved and a gasp caught in Cherrie's throat as the rags rolled to reveal two startling blue eyes.

It was a young girl, about sixteen years old. Cherrie continued to stare, mesmerised by her pale, pretty face. She was wearing a child's dress and its big blue checks reminded Cherrie of her school uniform which had been gathering dust in the wardrobe for the last two years. Something wasn't right, but Cherrie couldn't work it out.

Why was the girl on the floor? The dress was torn and dirty, but apart from her dishevelled look, there didn't seem to be anything wrong, until a small red stain began to spread across the cotton. Cherrie turned away.

"Help me. Help me please," it said.

Cherrie struggled to work out what was happening.

"It hurts. Please help."

She should call an ambulance. Cherrie reached for her bag, the small cross-over cotton square with the tassels that always clung to her side, but it wasn't there. She checked the other side, but it wasn't there either. Her memories were clouded as Cherrie desperately tried to remember. *Had she left her bag in the woods?* A distant humming began to register within her consciousness. Cherrie shivered, rubbing her arms for warmth. The deep, throaty rumble sounded like a lorry but, as it drew nearer, the noise became different; it was light and fast moving.

Cherrie ran. She ran away from the girl, pushing aside more pleas for help which drifted away across the woods. Crossing the lay-by, she reached the edge of the main road but, what had looked like a scrawny line of shrubs from a distance, were thick thorn bushes. She looked around, but the lay-by stretched far into the distance. The noise grew louder; time was running out and it would take too long to go around it. Cherrie covered her face with her arms and pushed her body through the thorns.

The noise was almost deafening. She ran straight into the road, facing the direction of the oncoming vehicle and waved her arms in large, circular movements. Her jeans had done a good job of protecting her legs from the thorns, but her t-shirt was ripped and her arms were speckled with blood. Cherrie felt ridiculous – a bedraggled eighteen year old making snow angels in the air. The last time it snowed, Cherrie had walked to school, only to discover it was closed. Everyone moaned about the inconvenience, but Cherrie enjoyed spending the day with her best friend, Mary and watching the kids down her street throwing snow balls.

The estate car flew around the bend. Cherrie saw the man behind the steering wheel and, for a moment, thought he would drive straight over her, but then the car swerved sharply into the oncoming lane. He didn't seem to be slowing down, but at the last minute, the green blur turned into the lay-by and drove back towards Cherrie, screeching to a stop almost opposite where she was standing. Only the thorny bushes separated them.

The man jumped out of the car. He was older than her dad, probably in his forties and dressed in ugly brown cords and a pullover. He was looking directly at Cherrie, but then he noticed the bundle on the verge.

"Holy crap." His voice drifted across to where Cherrie was standing. She watched him take a mobile phone from his trouser pocket and she listened to the desperation in his voice.

"Hello, I need an ambulance. There's a girl bleeding at the side of the road … yes it's the A614 … I don't know, somewhere near Ollerton, maybe. Please hurry."

He took off his pullover and placed it on top of the girl, hiding the blood. He took the girl's head in his hands and tenderly brushed the hair from her face.

"You're going to be okay. I'm right here," he said.

Cherrie had a good view through the bushes, which she'd dived into when the car stopped. Keeping low to the ground she held her breath and waited... Within minutes there were sirens and, as the noise grew louder, she heard a single word escape from the girl's lips before the lay-by filled with people, lights and noise.

"Angel."

Cherrie kept her distance, crouched and hiding amongst the thorns. She was close enough to hear their voices.

"Tell me again what happened?" the policeman said,

"A girl was standing in the road and flagged me down. I pulled over and then I saw her," he gestured the ambulance with his head, where the victim as she was now called, was being loaded through the back doors.

"So, it wasn't the victim who was in the road?"

"No, I already told the other officer. It was a different girl."

"Can you describe her?" The policeman flicked open his notebook.

"Well I only saw her for a minute. She was fairly ordinary with brown hair, wearing jeans and a black t-shirt with a star across the chest."

His pencil slid across the page.

"And where is she now?"

"I don't know. I was too busy trying to help the girl."

"Was she injured? The other girl, I mean."

"I don't know," the man sighed loudly. "I think there was blood on her arms."

"Did she say anything?"

"No, I mean yes. The girl in the road didn't speak, but the injured girl said 'Angel' that was all."

"What does that mean?"

"Look Officer, I've no idea."

The policeman closed his notebook. "There's no need to get agitated and it's Sergeant. Right, I need to carry out a breathalyser. Come with me."

The lay-by was busy, with three police cars, two black cars, the ambulance and the green car that belonged to the man. It had been sealed off at both entrances with thick, yellow tape to stop anyone else getting in. The Sergeant took the man over to one of the brightly decorated police cars. Cherrie felt sorry for him. The policeman seemed to be angry, but she couldn't work out why. Cherrie was tempted to crawl out of her hiding place and tell them to leave the man alone, but she didn't move. She had to hide. She couldn't remember why, but she knew she had to hide.

Two men filled the spot on the tarmac vacated by the policeman and the man. They were dressed in dark trousers, shirts and jackets and Cherrie wasn't sure who they were, but when they spoke, she realised they were also policemen. One man was older with grey hair and the other was young and blonde; they were just like the detectives on television.

"What do you think, is he telling the truth, Sir?"

"It's unlikely he'd stab her and then call us, but not impossible."

"I'm guessing that's his jumper covered in blood." The young detective gestured to the discarded pullover, the ambulance woman had removed from the girl.

"He covered her up with it. It's perfectly reasonable, Sparks."

"Yes Sir. Do you think there might be a connection to the missing girls?"

"Not likely, but you can have a look around if you want to."

"Want me to call in the dogs to search the woods?"

"No, just have a quick look around and shout if you see anything dodgy."

"Thank you Sir."

The girl was stabbed, that's what the detective said. As he spoke Cherrie visualised a knife with a thick, red plastic handle, she didn't know why. All the knives at home had slender black handles and belonged to a set that her mother

180

had been given. A siren bounced through the air and Cherrie watched as the ambulance pulled away, stopping briefly for a policeman to drag the yellow tape aside. Cherrie hoped the girl would be okay. As she watched the ambulance disappear, another vehicle materialised, accompanied by a low rumble. Cherrie was mesmerised as the lorry slowed and the driver diverted his gaze across the flashing lights of the police cars. At that moment Cherrie remembered; she remembered everything.

It was another bright day. She was walking along the road with her arms dangling loosely by her sides and listening to the rustle of the wind, but it wasn't the noise she was hoping to hear. The late afternoon sunshine wasn't able to keep her warm and Cherrie wished she had a jacket with her. She instinctively side stepped a large pot hole and counted ten paces forward to the next one. The route was familiar, but it took her a while to work it out as her memory seemed to be misfiring lately. It was the road which led to Mary's house – her best friend.

Cherrie's mind drifted to thoughts of Mary. *How long had she been missing?* It must have been more than a month since they'd walked this road together. The roar of the engine approached at speed, closing in on her position quicker than she thought and, for a moment, Cherrie worried that she'd missed her chance. Eagerly she extended her bare arm and willed her hand to form the "thumbs up" position. It seemed to require much more effort than usual, but he must have seen her because the roar changed to a squeal and the lorry shuddered to a stop a few feet in front of her. She walked the length of the vehicle and, as she arrived at the passenger door, it flung open. She heaved her frame up the high step and hovered in the doorway.

"I'm looking for a ride."

"Hop in sweetheart."

Cherrie didn't need any further encouragement. She eased into the seat and pulled on the heavy door.

"Here let me," he said and reached across her to pull the door shut.

He didn't ask where she wanted to go, but simply started the engine and began to drive. Cherrie didn't speak; she already knew their destination. A curiosity arose within her and she found that she was staring at him, recalling some of his features like the well-rounded belly and shaved head, but seeing others for the first time. The radio was playing quietly in the background and she wondered whether she should turn it up. *Would the music be a cover for his screams or would it attract more attention?*

He kept his focus on the road, appearing to concentrate on manoeuvring the lorry through the twists and turns. Cherrie patiently waited for the right moment. When they were only a few miles from the woodland, she edged her fingers along the grimy fabric and reached down into the space between the two seats. A silky tassel brushed her skin and Cherrie gasped, remembering her lovely lilac bag. She quickly pushed the tassel to one side and kept feeling around until the cold, metal object was firmly in her grasp. It was just where she remembered it. Carefully she teased it upwards and slowly eased it behind her back, all the while focusing on the road ahead as if she was just another hitch hiker along for a ride.

He pulled the lorry into the lay-by. It was the same one which a day earlier had been surrounded by police tape and Cherrie silently thanked the part of human nature which craved familiarity; it would make things much easier.

"I just need a piss, won't be a mo," he was already jumping out of the cab.

Cherrie could see the woods through her side window but, instead of crossing in front of the cab, he disappeared around the back of the lorry. She glanced at the spot on her door where the mirror would usually give a view along the passenger side of the vehicle, but she already knew it was missing. Taking a deep breath, she pulled the knife out from behind her back; she was ready.

The passenger door swung open and a rush of cool air filled the cab. In spite of being prepared, Cherrie was momentarily startled. She gripped the knife in her shaking hand, but it wasn't until he reached out to grab her that Cherrie thrust it at him. She was aiming for his heart, but she missed and the blade sank into his shoulder.

"What the...?" he looked confused.

Cherrie pulled out the knife and thrust it at him again, this time driving it firmly into his chest. She had expected him to fall, but he stood firm, only inches away from her. Her tiny fingers clutched the thick, red plastic handle and Cherrie withdrew the blade from his flesh.

"Don't you remember me?" her voice quivered as she spoke.

He shook his head, dazed by what was happening. Blood began to spread across his t-shirt and Cherrie wanted to look away, but she knew she couldn't, not this time.

"Where's Mary?" she demanded.

"What did you do, you mad bitch?"

"You almost killed me, you're the evil bastard. Now, where's my friend?"

"I don't know what you're talking about, love."

He was stubborn and Cherrie's anger took hold. She stabbed him twice more before she saw the wild fires glare in his eyes and she moved away from him, settling into the driver's seat. She watched as he clung to his chest, the blood raining down his clothes.

"Who are you?" his words were quiet and feeble.

Cherrie didn't answer; this wasn't how she'd envisaged it. In her version, he remembered the evil that he had done, told her where to find her friend and begged for her forgiveness.

She opened the driver's door and walked around the front of the cab. By the time she reached him, he'd collapsed on the grass verge a few feet from where the girl in the blue dress had bled, but this time it was his blood seeping into the foliage. His breaths were noisy, there were tears in his eyes and blood was starting to trickle from the corner of his mouth.

"Where is she? Please tell me where to find my friend."

He didn't even try to respond.

Cherrie looked at the sharp steel which she still clutched in her hand, but her strength had evaporated. She dropped the knife and walked away, leaving him gasping and bleeding at the side of the lay-by.

The lay-by was awash with flashing lights and loud voices. Uniformed men and women scurried around and Cherrie thought it looked like a scene from a film. She wasn't sure how long she'd been standing at the edge of the woodland, but she watched from the comfort of the trees, as the crew loaded the man into the back of the ambulance. *Was he breathing?* She couldn't tell and although she mostly hoped he was dead, there was a small part of her which hoped he was alive. He hadn't confessed his sins to her, but maybe he would tell the police and then she could find Mary. She listened intently as three familiar faces positioned themselves at the edge of the woods and stared into the darkness.

"Did he say anything, Sergeant?" the senior detective asked.

"Not much, just something about a girl and stars. He was barely conscious."

"Will he live?"

"Doc wasn't sure. Said he'd been stabbed four or five times."

"And you found the knife?"

"Yes, about two feet from the body."

"Thank you Sergeant, that's all for now."

"Okay Sir."

The uniformed officer re-joined his colleagues who were going through the lorry on the far side of the lay-by, leaving the two detectives within a few feet of where Cherrie was hiding. She had a headache and was starting to feel queasy, but she couldn't walk away. She clung to the rough bark of a tree and listened intently to the voices of the two men. Although she felt weak, she tried hard to concentrate on what was happening...

"Did he say stars? Hmm that sounds familiar." Sparks started flicking through his notebook.

"Didn't the witness yesterday claim he saw a girl in a star t-shirt?"

"Yes, here it is." The junior detective looked up from his notebook.

"Well, I think 'Star Girl' might be worth finding, what did the victim say?"

"She's still unconscious, but the witness reported her saying the word "angel" before she passed out. What do you think Sir?"

"Well Sparks, I think we might have a female killer on the loose."

"Sir," a voice from across the lay-by was swiftly followed by the panting of a policeman in a hurry to reach the two men. "We found something."

"Slow down and tell me exactly what you found, Sergeant."

"Girls things, I mean things that might belong to the missing girls."

"You're assuming that…" Sparks interrupted.

"There was a whole load of things under the passenger seat in the cab – a hair comb, a headscarf and a bag with blood all over it."

"Was there any identification in the bag?" the senior detective asked.

"I don't know Sir, I didn't look. Do you think the lorry driver is our abductor?"

"I don't know Sergeant, but two stabbings on the same bit of road in two days seems a bit coincidental. Call in the dogs; let's make a start searching the woods and check that bag for ID."

Cherrie was still watching as the ambulance departed and uniformed officers began to spread out along the length of the lay-by. Under instructions from the senior detective, they began to advance towards the woods. As they approached the edge of the tree-line one of the policemen was only a few feet away from Cherrie. She held her breath, but he walked right past as if she wasn't there. She decided to follow at what she judged to be a safe distance. They had advanced about fifty feet when the junior detective shouted.

"Over here, Sir."

Cherrie watched as the two detectives and a couple of policemen crowded around a clump of nettles and dipped their heads, as if in prayer. *What were they looking at?* It was dark in the woods and she couldn't see clearly. She quietly moved in closer and, in the gloom, Cherrie caught sight of a shape. It was a body – the body of a girl, lying on its back with the face covered in dirt. Sparks reached down and gently brushed the earth away to reveal soft, pale skin.

Tidal waves of emotion embraced Cherrie as she recognised the lifeless body of her best friend. They had found Mary, but it was too late to save her. Memories had started to come back when the girl in the blue dress had pleaded for her help. Cherrie had suddenly remembered the lorry, the man and persuading Mary to accept a lift.

"Come on it will be fun," she had said as she pulled Mary into the cab.

Cherrie wasn't usually reckless but she thought they'd be safe, after all there were two of them and he was just an overweight driver. Didn't everyone hitch hike at their age?

"Oh fuck!"

The words jolted Cherrie from her thoughts. She wasn't sure who had spoken, but the policemen were now crowded around another bump in the earth, only a couple of feet away from Mary. Cherrie watched as they pushed the earth away from their new discovery. It was another body and this one was also strangely familiar.

"Braithwaite, Sir." The Sergeant interrupted the mourners and handed the senior detective a photo driving licence.

"Where did you find this Sergeant?"

"It was in the bag. The one we found under the passenger seat."

"I remember that name," the junior detective flicked through his notebook. "One of the missing girls is called Braithwaite."

The senior detective bent down and held the licence against the face of the second body. "Well she's not missing anymore."

187

"Yes, here it is, Cherrie Braithwaite. She was last seen with best friend, Mary Richmond."

As soon as he said her name, Cherrie recognised her face amongst the nettles. She watched as he brushed the dirt from her clothes. She loved those black jeans and the t-shirt had been a present. She thought it was a bit childish, I mean sequins were a bit 1970s, but she had grown to love the silver star-shape. Cherrie wanted to cry, but she didn't have the energy. She was having problems hearing what the detectives were saying, but it no longer seemed to matter; then there was a new voice.

"Cherrie." It called out to her. "Cherrie, I'm over here."

Cherrie turned and in the distance she saw her. Suddenly the heaviness in her limbs was lifted and her energy was restored. She ran through the woods as fast as she could, skipping over the fallen branches and jumping through the dead leaves until she reached her.

"Where've you been?"

"I was trying to find you," Cherrie said.

"I've been waiting for ages."

"I'm sorry Mary, but I'm here now."

Cherrie threw her arms around her best friend and hugged her tightly.

"C'mon let's go," Mary said.

"No! Let's go this way."

Cherrie grabbed Mary and pulled her away, away from the police, away from the lay-by and away from the past. She wasn't going to leave her friend again and she kept a firm grip on Mary's hand as they skipped towards the sunshine together.

Dedication
To my grandparents who were wonderful people

Katie is currently studying an MA in Creative Writing. She is interested in romance, science fiction and thrillers, and several of her short stories have been published in magazines and anthologies. Although studying takes up most of her time, she hopes to finish her first novel next year.

Warm Breeze

Laura Wilkinson

He blew in with the spring. Budding daffodils, crisp skies, or so I'd heard from those who cared. I hadn't bothered to look out of the window. I spent all my time in bed, refusing to get up, to speak even.

He appeared on a Tuesday. I knew it was Tuesday because there were boiled eggs and toast on my untouched breakfast tray. I was suffering my regular rotation, mechanically turned, like a hog on a spit, suspended in mid-air looking down at the blind white sheets of my bed. The turning stops the bed sores, apparently.

"I can see your knickers," a male voice said.

"Good for you," I said, annoyed, because I hadn't meant to reply. I'd been silent for days. Perhaps it was his belligerent tone.

"You're not bothered then? That anyone gliding by can see your pants."

"I couldn't give a damn."

"You're very pretty."

"What?"

"You're lovely. What's your name?" he said.

"Get stuffed." In my head I heard my mother tut-tutting.

"Mine's Nigel," he said, "nice to meet you too." And then he was gone, and I was alone once more.

Such an ordinary name.

The next time he came I was sat up in bed, pretending to read one of my set books. I couldn't see the point in studying for A levels now, but I kept up appearances to stop my mum nagging. The squeak of tyres splintered the hushed hospital air and I knew it was him. I kept my eyes locked to the page.

"Hello, beautiful. What you reading?"

"None of your business." I could see the bottom of his wheels in my peripheral vision. His aftershave filled the air, though I couldn't pinpoint the scent; it was quite unlike anything I'd ever smelt before.

"I'd love to read a book, a magazine, anything, but it's difficult to hold things between your teeth and focus." He had my attention now; I looked up.

His eyes were green, his hair strawberry blonde. He was older than me by five or six years: twenty-two or three. Not what you'd call good-looking, but interesting, unusual. And quadriplegic. It should have made me feel better, someone worse off than me, but it made me angry, though that was okay. At least I was feeling something.

He looked like he was waiting for a reply, and I realised I'd been staring. The blood rushed to my cheeks.

"What happened to you?" he said.

"I came off my motorbike."

"How?"

"I dunno. It was dark, I hit the brakes too hard, maybe there was oil on the road."

"Was it like being in slow motion?"

"Was it hell."

"What do you remember?"

I have no idea why I told him. I'd not spoken to anyone about it until then. I was thrown over a cliff and into the branch of a tree. A battered, hillside tree that saved my life and broke my spine. At the waist. No hope of repair. I remembered dangling there, looking at my feet, one boot missing.

Time rolled on; the dawn broke. Then: "Helloooooo? Hellooooo? Anybody there?" A strong Welsh accent pattered down the hillside like spring rain.

"I'm in a tree, I came off my bike."

"I know love, I saw it, on the verge, I did. Wondered where it came from. Thought someone might be hurt I did, I was driving down to the market I was…"

"Get help," I yelled.

"Okay, lovey. I'll call the fire brigade I will. Straight away, right now. You sit tight. No need to worry. An ambulance too I think."

"Yes, and get a bloody move on you stupid old bugger." I didn't say the last bit out loud of course. I saw him as a middle-aged farmer, ruddy of cheek, quick of hand and slow of mind.

"Were you always so angry?" Nigel asked. He looked kind of old-fashioned, a bit dated, in his Adidas t-shirt, stone-washed jeans and Cuban-heeled boots. His chest was broad – like his shoulders and upper arms had done a lot of work – and I wondered how tall he was, and tried to imagine him standing upright but couldn't.

He said, "What did it feel like? Did you know?"

I said, "I knew my life was over. I felt a thud in my back, then a lunging forwards and backwards, bouncing. I felt the branch adjusting to the weight of its new leaf."

"You're very poetic. Must be all that reading."

"What happened to you?" I asked, throwing my hair over my shoulders, suddenly conscious of my shapeless hospital gown.

"I dived into a wave at Abersoch."

"No kidding."

"Yeah, unbelievable isn't it? If the force is just so, and if it hits your neck in just the right spot, then, bingo! You lose the use of everything from the shoulders down. I am a talking head."

I asked how long he'd been here.

"Forever," he said, smiling.

"What on earth possessed you to go swimming in Tremadog Bay?" I said. "It's freezing."

"I was practising for a channel swim." He smiled, and I noticed that his teeth were really white; they gave off a blinding light. Hypnotic. "Tell me your name."

"Siân."

"Mine's Nigel."

"You said."

"So you were listening." He winked.

"Nice to meet you, Nigel," I said. And I meant it.

He came to see me every day. Not always at the same time, so I lived with a permanent air of expectation. The waiting was such an intense form of pleasure it felt like pain. Even the dozy nurses noticed the difference in me. I stopped cutting.

I'd been in hospital six weeks before I looked at my legs. When I did, I was surprised they hadn't altered. I'd expected them to wither instantly, to look crumbled and useless. I poked them repeatedly, willing a response, and when it never came I took to cutting my thighs. Small cuts at first, then deeper and deeper, as if I was digging for treasure, the jewel: sensation. Stealing the knife was easier than it should have been.

The blood startled me at first. I hadn't expected those pathetic limbs to bleed. The cutting was another thing I found myself telling Nigel.

Visiting time, and Mum ranted on and on. "You don't mix, the nurses tell me. You talk to yourself. You're withdrawn and sullen. It's not healthy, Siân."

Head down, I remained silent while she harassed, but when she began to cry I took hold of her hand and mentioned, as casually as I could, that, in fact, I had made a friend. She wiped her face with both hands, smearing

193

lipstick as well as dribbled mascara across her cheeks and said, "About bloody time. Tell me all about her."

"Him."

Eyebrows arched she asked all sorts of questions and I realised how little I knew about him. But what he did for a living, who his parents were, where he lived, all that shit, none of it mattered; we were soul mates.

"Can I tell your friends they can visit?" Mum said.

"I'm not ready. Don't want them to see me like this."

"Oh Siân."

She looked like a clown with her face all smudged like that, but she was happy, I could tell, and just for a moment I acted happy too. Evidently, she was so happy with my news she blathered to the nurses.

"Found a reason to get out of bed, have we, dear? Nothing to do with the mysterious Nigel, I suppose?" one of them teased.

"I'd keep quiet if I were you," I said, "otherwise you can say goodbye to me getting out of bed."

"I preferred it when you were mute, Siân." She was trying to be funny, so I smiled. She was much older than the others; she reminded me of my mum: always fussing, incessant chatter, kind. No wonder they got on well. But the only person I felt normal with, real, like I didn't have to put on a performance, was Nigel.

The weeks rolled by. I was in the day room, sitting at the back, frittering time when Nigel appeared.

"Christ! You made me jump. Didn't hear you come in."

A chorus of "Sssshhh!" reverberated. A popular soap opera was on the telly.

Nigel looked round the room. He whispered, "I spy with my little eye something beginning with 'c'."

194

"Cripple!" I shouted, and an orderly fiddling with the remote control glared at me.

"What are you staring at?" I barked. "I can call myself whatever I sodding well like, it's only you lot who can walk who can't say cripple – cripple! Cripples! We're all bloody cripples!" A few inmates shook their heads, others chuckled. An old bloke a few metres in front of me turned to his neighbour and said, "Bad case that one. Always jabbering, shouting out. Completely bonkers."

I was about to ask him what the hell he was talking about when Nigel said, "Leave it, Siân."

Some days I felt like a piece of bread floating in a kerbside puddle, slowly disintegrating. Even Nigel found it difficult to make me smile then, and self-absorbed as I was it didn't occur to me that he might feel the same.

Easter came. He brought me an enormous chocolate bunny.

"I'll get fat," I said, embarrassed, and wishing I'd asked Mum to get an extra egg for him.

"You'll suit a size twelve chair," he said, tapping his chin on the chair controls. He whizzed away before I could thank him.

We spent more and more time together. We didn't always talk; we'd watch the telly, play stupid guessing games, or simply park our chairs outside and stare at the clouds. He allowed me to rage, to rail against the pity and suffocating kindness.

Family and friends found it difficult when I tried to talk about how useless and cheated I felt. I couldn't moan about anything; I had to be the cheerful little cripple, grateful to be alive when most of the time I wished I was dead. That the bloody tree hadn't caught me.

But Nigel understood. He was my comrade fighting

off the cloying love of the able-bodied army. He rode with me into battle; we flew along endless corridors, channelling rage through our wheels.

Often I'd feel his presence before I saw him. He seemed to know exactly when I needed him; he'd materialise when the fog of nothingness descended, like soft lamplight, leading me through it, encouraging me to feel. Something. Anything. Anger came easiest, though he turned it to laughter with an ease that verged on the miraculous.

Summer approached and little moments of everyday joy crept up on me: the smell of cooking bacon from the kitchens, the crispness of freshly laundered sheets, a purple nail varnish Mum bought me. I longed to share these moments with Nigel, but whenever I felt content, or happy, he was nowhere to be seen.

During one such spell I went looking for him and after searching in all the obvious places, without success, I asked a member of staff.

"And which friend would this be then, Siân?" the nurse said.

I shook my head, uncomprehending, irritation rising. I had only one mate here. She continued, "We're worried about you, Siân. You spend so much time alone, you need to mix, get out there. You'll be leaving before you know it. Not long now."

"I'm fine," I said, spinning on my wheels, abandoning her mid-sentence, not listening, the bad feelings resurfacing.

Nigel was waiting in my room. "You're almost ready. It's time I was off," he said.

"You've got a discharge date?" Panic rose in my gut. How would I cope here without him?

"Not exactly," he said, "but soon. Soon I'll be gone."

There was a heaviness to his words, like a lump was forming in his throat. Then he changed the subject and we fell about laughing, metaphorically speaking, about something or other.

Four days later we sat on the lawn counting daisies. We had a wager. A flock of birds danced overhead – starlings I think – swooping down, then up again, a dark, shifting mass. Like clouds of ash blowing in the wind. The rush of air swirling around my head reminded me of riding my bike. I looked at the birds and said, "It was the closest I ever got to flying, on the bike. With the wind in my face, air rushing round my limbs, I felt like I rode above the rest of the world. It was an incredible feeling – like true, unrivalled freedom. If that makes sense? I'd like to have learnt how to fly. Or hand gliding or something. Was swimming like that for you? Entering another world, another dimension?"

"Diving was. THE dive for definite. Oh, this bloody wind," Nigel said.

Sorrow and loss clutched my throat and held tight, squeezing harder and harder. I thought of everything I'd miss: climbing stairs two at a time, the sting in the thighs afterwards, warm sand running through my toes. I had not cried. I had cradled and nurtured my anger; I'd forgotten how to be sad. Or maybe the fury had burnt the reservoir dry. And I had not seen Nigel cry or confess that he had.

"I've got a hair in my eye – bloody wind!" he said, moving his head from side to side like a dog with a bucket on its head trying to lick a wound on its haunches.

I couldn't speak.

There were no nurses around. There was rarely anyone about when Nigel was present. I circled round until my back wheel was flush against his front. I looked into his eye, framed by sandy lashes, and then into his face. He

197

was so vulnerable. I'd never seen him like that. He always appeared so robust, so vital. He reminded me of a Viking. I could see him rampaging his way across unknown lands. Red veins cracked along the whites of his watering eye. The iris was clear and green and lovely, and as I pulled at the rogue hair my hand brushed his cheek and the tears came. And I couldn't stop them.

I wanted to pull away, but I couldn't tear my face from his. The light behind his eyes drew me in and I leant forward. Forehead to forehead I grieved my able-bodied life. I felt his skin, soft like feathers, against the tip of my nose and though our lips touched we didn't kiss.

The next day he appeared as I sat at the back of the day room pretending to watch that shitty soap opera. I'd wanted people around me. Nigel whispered, "On the lawn yesterd—"

"Sorry about that. I was a bit of an idiot."

"I was dying to kiss you, Siân."

I wished he had; I'd wanted it so badly it hurt. But I said, "You're kidding me?"

"I'm not. But I'm glad I didn't."

"Oh," I said.

"It's against regulations. I'd be breaking all the rules." I felt sure that had he been able, he'd have shrugged.

I was confused and didn't get what he meant by regulations. There was nothing to stop inmates having relationships, it was a hospital, not a bloody monastery, and I was about to say so when someone parked near the window turned and asked me to stop muttering. I stared at the telly. Perhaps friendship was best.

"Something's changed for me," I whispered. "A new beginning, life feels like life again."

"You're healed then," Nigel said, not looking at me.

"A new life. It began yesterday," I said, smiling.

198

"No, it didn't. It began the second you hit the branch. It began the second you decided not to fall from that tree, to hang on, to live. You just didn't know it till now. My task is complete; you no longer need me."

I kissed him on the cheek. His skin felt powdery, like dust.

"Steady, girl. Steady."

"You're wrong, I do need you. We'll always be friends."

He didn't reply.

I said, "I'm going to learn how to drive, get a special car. I'll visit."

"You'll meet the right man someday." He stared straight ahead then turned his chair to leave.

"And you'll find a girlfriend. It needn't get in the way," I called after him, pushing at my wheels.

"Will you shut up?" another patient spat, rolling his finger in a circular motion at the side of his head.

I stuck out my tongue as I wheeled past. I caught up with Nigel in the corridor.

He said, "There'll be other assignments, other girls. Maybe not as pretty as you, but sunnier, nowhere near as crabby."

"You cheeky sod."

He sped up; I couldn't keep pace. I watched him disappear down the corridor, his wheels lifting off the ground as if he was flying, fading to dust, like a sooty, amorphous mass of starlings.

I never did see Nigel again. For days I asked after him, but no one seemed to have heard of him, let alone seen him. In the end I spoke with the old nurse, the one that reminded me of Mum. She recalled a young man, a boy she called him, who'd been brought to the hospital years ago after a diving accident. His spinal chord had been severed, at the neck. He clung onto life for only a few days after contracting pneumonia. "It was all too much for him in the end," she said, "his poor, battered body just couldn't take it."

She touched the corner of her eye with her finger, like she was wiping away a tear or removing a speck of dust. "But his name wasn't Nigel, dear. It was Raphael, like the angel."

Dedication
Warm Breeze is dedicated to Pete Burrows

Laura Wilkinson grew up in Wales and now lives in Brighton. Recently, she's worked as a freelance writer, an editor and a copywriter. In between raising her two young boys and working she's polishing her second novel. She's had short stories published in magazines. This story first appeared in the Spring 2011 edition of Scribble magazine, awarded 'Best Short Fiction Magazine 2007' by Writers' Grand Circle: www.parkpublications.co.uk.

Laura's début novel, *BloodMining* won the Debut Novel Competition and was published by Bridge House in October 2011.

www.laura-wilkinson.co.uk
http://twitter.com/#ScorpioScribble

Index of Authors

Other Publications by Bridge House

BloodMining

by Laura WIlkinson

Megan Evens appears to have it all: brains, beauty, a success-
ful career as a foreign correspondent. But deep down she is
lonely and rootless. Pregnant, craving love but unable to trust
after the destructive affair with her baby's father she returns to
the security of her birthplace in Wales.

When Megan's son is later diagnosed with a terminal condition, a degenerative, hereditary disease, everything she
believed to be true about her origins is thrown into question.
To save her son Megan must unearth the truth; she must
excavate family history and memory. Enlisting the help of
former colleague Jack North, a man with a secret of his own,
Megan embarks on a journey of self discovery and into the
heart of what it means to be a parent.

"Lean, lyrical, topical and emotionally gripping. This book is
about the issues that we care about most – with a twist. Read it
and pass on the word!"
Yvonne Roberts, award-winning journalist and author

Order from www.bridgehousepublishing.co.uk

978-1-907335-14-3

Calling for Angels
by Alex Smith

Em tries to avoid the annoying clones – the girls in her year at Philiton Comprehensive who spend all their time thinking about clothes, make-up and boys. She worries about her aging grandparents and her older brother Ollie, who seems to be behaving in a distinctly odd way.

Then three new people come into her life: the mysterious woman who gives her a beautifully carved figurine, Kai whose own story has a touch of sadness, and Zak, the new guy who causes a stir amongst the girls.

And she discovers she needs to call for angels.

Alex Smith is 16 and lives in Hertfordshire, England. She started writing when she was just four and says, "to me, writing is like breathing." She finished her debut novel, Calling For Angels, at the age of 14, "as a way of relaxing".

Winner of *The Red Telephone's* 2009 novel competition.

Order from http://theredtelephone.co.uk
The Red Telephone – an imprint of Bridge House

ISBN 978-1-907335-09-9

Hipp-O-Dee-Doo-Dah

You'll find all sorts of animals in this collection of stories – a hippo who longs for water, a chimp that proves to be tougher than a gorilla, a horse only two people can see, a cat that cooks, a starfish that falls from the sky and dogs that save lives.

There are some amazing people too – the young girl who looks after her mum, some young people who have magical powers they have to hide, a boy who finds a new way to remember his grandfather, and a young man who has the universe at his command but daren't let others see.

All of the stories are about how people are thoughtful with each other or with the animals in their care. And they'll bring sunshine to a grey day.

Hipp-O-Dee-Doo-Dah features stories by Blue Peter Award winners Lauren St John and Alan Gibbons, and a foreword by Michael Morpurgo OBE.

£1 from the sale of each copy, plus a percentage of the author royalties, will be donated to Children's Hospices UK.

Order from www.bridgehousepublishing.co.uk

ISBN 978-1-907335-11-2

Gentle Footprints

Gentle Footprints is a wonderful collection of short stories about wild animals. The stories are fictional but each story gives a real sense of the wildness of the animal, true to the Born Free edict that animals should be born free and should live free. The animals range from the octopus to the elephant, each story beautifully written.

Gentle Footprints includes a new and highly original story by Richard Adams, author of *Watership Down*, and a foreword by the patron of Born Free, Virginia McKenna OBE.

£1 from the sale of each copy, plus a percentage of the author royalties, will be donated to The Born Free Foundation.

This special book will raise both awareness and much-needed funds for the animals. Check out the Gentle Footprints blog which includes links and information from Born Free about each of the featured animals. Find out how you can get involved in their conservation:
http://gentlefootprintsanimalanthology.blogspot.com

Order from www.bridgehousepublishing.co.uk

ISBN 978-1-907335-04-4

Critiquing and Mentoring
Service for Budding Writers

If this collection has inspired you and if you have a stack of short stories or the start of a novel crammed away in a drawer and you want to do something with it, I can help.

As a featured author, editor and marketing manager for Bridge House Publishing I offer good rates on short story critiques and also a new mentoring scheme.

Check out my website for more information:
www.debzhobbs-wyatt.co.uk

Do you have a short story in you?

Then why not have a go at one of our competitions or try your hand at a story for one of our anthologies? Check out:

http://bridgehousepublishing.co.uk/competition.aspx

Submissions

Bridge House publishes books which are a little bit different, such as *Making Changes*, *In the Shadow of the Red Queen* and *Alternative Renditions*.

We are particularly keen to promote new writers and believe that our approach is friendly and supportive to encourage those who may not have been published previously. We are also interested in published writers and welcome submissions from all authors who believe they have a story that would tie into one of our themed anthologies.

Full details about submissions process, and how to submit your work to us for consideration, can be found on our website

http://bridgehousepublishing.co.uk/newsubmissions.aspx

Lightning Source UK Ltd.
Milton Keynes UK
UKOW05f2029290913

218146UK00002B/95/P